THE RISING

THE RISING

SAM HOUSTON
BOOK TWO

ROBERT WISEHART

WOLFPACK
PUBLISHING
— EST 2013 —

Wolfpack Publishing
1707 E. Diana Street
Tampa, FL 33610

www.wolfpackpublishing.com

Paperback ISBN 979-8-89567-732-2
Ebook ISBN 979-8-89567-768-1

THE RISING

THE RISING

1

GENERAL! General! They're dead! They're all dead!

Sam Houston jumped up from the portable desk where he was trying to think of a diplomatic way to tell the political leadership of Texas that it was rife with damn fools, opened the flap of his tent, and glared out at the commotion.

The offender was a youngster of maybe fifteen years, astride a horse that looked like it belonged in front of a plow. Houston recognized him as one of Deaf Smith's messengers, which made him someone to be listened to. A crowd had already started to gather, curious about who was dead.

"This is an army camp, not a revival," Houston snapped. "Shut your mouth, get off that farm animal, and come in here."

The chastened boy slid off the horse and approached the tent like it was a firing squad. Houston turned on his heel and went back inside, confident that the messenger would follow.

Houston resumed his place on the three-legged stool. "Keep your voice down," he instructed, his tone gentle this time. "Erastus gave you a message for me, didn't he?"

A confused look crossed the youngster's face before he realized that "Erastus" was his superior, the man everyone called Deaf Smith, though they pronounced it "Deef." Houston preferred his real name, Erastus, or sometimes Mister E, figuring that a man of Smith's talents deserved respect.

The enlightened messenger nodded, brushing back the tangled blonde hair that flopped down over his eyes.

"What is it?" Houston prodded.

It came out in a confused burst.

"There's a woman on a mule and a baby and Travis' boy named Joe. Deaf found 'em on the road out of Bear. He's bringin' 'em in now. She says they're dead, every last one."

If Houston understood the garbled message, Smith had discovered a woman and a baby riding a mule somewhere on the road out of San Antonio de Bexar, which most Texians called Bear, along with somebody named Joe who claimed to be Buck Travis' slave or servant.

"Who's dead?" Houston asked, knowing the answer he was likely to get and afraid of it right down to his toes. "Who did they say was dead?"

"The Alamo ... every mother's son."

It took all of Houston's self control to keep his face steady and unrevealing. The Alamo had to fall. Every report and messenger only reinforced the notion. There was no way around it. But every defender dead? He steepled his fingers in front of his chin and tried to think it through. There wasn't much time. Best keep it quiet for as long as he could. Once panic started in a camp like this it was impossible to stop.

"I want you to get back on that horse and find Erastus. Tell him to bring the woman here but wait till dark. Tell him to come the back way and walk the last bit so they won't draw attention. Tell him not to say a word to anyone."

Houston rose to his full height of six feet, two inches so that he towered over the intimidated boy.

"That order applies to you, too. You will speak to no one

except Erastus. Understand? If I hear you blabbed to anyone else, I will have you skinned."

Receiving a frightened nod in reply, Houston barked, "Now git!"

Once the messenger mounted his plow horse and plodded away, Houston fell to the stool and cradled his head in his hands, the heels of his palms digging into his eyes. He desperately hoped that his chief scout was wrong.

But Erastus Smith was never wrong.

2

THEY ARRIVED about an hour after sundown.

Following instructions, they entered camp quietly and on foot so that the few who noticed didn't know what they saw. Houston was half convinced that if the need arose the canny Smith could make himself invisible.

With Houston, the scout, the woman, and her baby, the tent was crowded, but it would have to do. If ever there was a need for privacy, it was now. Besides, Houston knew that it would help bring Smith into the conversation. He wasn't really deaf, just hard of hearing from some childhood sickness. The closer you were the better he heard, especially if he faced you.

"Ma'am, please take a seat," Houston said, guiding the exhausted woman to his cot. He could feel her weakness through his arm around her waist. Gratefully, she sank down on the cot, hiking the baby a little higher so that her shoulder and not her arms took most of the weight.

"May I offer you some refreshment?" Houston asked. "Water, or some spirits?"

4

Looking up from the depths of exhaustion, she replied, "Do you have any milk for my baby? It's been too long."

"Hockley!"

Houston's spade-bearded aide, George Washington Hockley, stuck his head in through the closed tent flap.

"Sir?"

"Find some milk for the babe here."

"Milk?" asked thunderstruck the young man. "Here?"

"Yes, milk. It's white and comes out of a cow teat. And maybe a little bread to soak in the milk." Seeing the woman's approval, Houston added, "Go find it."

Hockley frowned and pulled his head out of the tent. Houston didn't blame him for the frown. He had no idea where to find milk in this piddling excuse for a camp, which is why he had Hockley do it.

Knowing that the woman would be more at ease once her baby was properly tended to, Houston waited for the milk to appear while she cooed to the child. It gave him the opportunity to assess her out of the corner of his eye.

Shine her up and she might be reasonably good-looking, he decided, but it would take a lot of shining up. Her bare feet were filthy and her skirt was torn into rags, revealing more of her legs than society would normally allow. Her dark eyes were tortured hollows and her cheekbones were too prominent on her face, a sign that she'd lost more weight than was good for her. With all the dirt, it was hard to tell the color of her hair. Houston guessed light brown.

As time passed, the silence became awkward. "I'm sure Hockley will be here directly with the milk," Houston said, offering assurance that he did not feel.

But no sooner did he say the words than Hockley miraculously appeared with a pitcher half full of warm milk in one hand and a few crusts of bread in the other.

Accepting the milk and bread, Houston ordered, "Stay outside and keep watch. We are not to be interrupted."

It took no time at all for the hungry baby to devour most of two crusts soaked in milk. A few moments after that, she was asleep in her mother's arms.

While the baby was fed, Houston had a whispered conversation with Smith, remembering to face him directly so the scout could tell what he was saying.

"What happened to the slave?"

"Run off," Smith whispered in reply, ruffling his thin gray hair with one hand. "I could have run him down easy enough but I didn't want to waste the time. It don't matter anyway. I got everything out of him he had to give. Tell you about it when you're finished with the lady."

Houston nodded, knowing Smith's word was good. Taking his place on the stool, with the scout standing beside him, he said, "Ma'am, I know this will be painful, but we need to know what happened. I'm sure you told some of it to Erastus, but now I need to hear it all. What you tell us could help decide the fate of our new nation."

"New nation?" she asked, puzzled at the phrase.

"Just a few days ago, over at Washington-on-the-Brazos," Houston explained. "Texas declared its independence on March second; my birthday, as a matter of fact. That's one reason why I was delayed getting' here. Even at that, I left before all the details were worked out; the new President, the cabinet and such. They're chewin' on that now."

"Now please," he urged. "Tell me what happened."

She shook her head, careful not to disturb the baby. "There's so much. I don't know where to start."

"Why don't you tell me who you are?"

She lifted her chin and Houston saw pride peak through the grime. "My name is Susannah Dickinson. My husband is Almeron Dickinson. This is our child, Angelina."

With a jolt, Houston realized that he knew her husband, or at least knew who he was. He hadn't expected a familiar name. A genial man with the muscled arms and broad shoulders of the blacksmith that he was, Dickinson had served in the regular army back in Tennessee, if Houston remembered it right, and he came out of it with a fair knowledge of cannon. If Houston ever met the man's wife, the woman sitting before him now, he didn't recall it.

"We were in Bear, livin' at the Musquiz house. Almeron was part of the garrison, about a hundred men. Jim Bowie came ridin' in with a few men and then Buck Travis showed up with a few more. It made a hundred and fifty, or so, they said."

She stopped and searched her memory. "It might have been the other way 'round; Travis then Bowie. I can't remember."

Houston reached across the space between them and touched her elbow.

"It doesn't matter. You're doin' fine. Please, go on."

Houston knew all about Bowie going to Bexar. He was the one who sent him, intending that Bowie save what ordnance he could, blow up the Alamo so Santa Anna couldn't use it as a base, and rejoin the army. Instead, after only a few days Bowie and Travis sent out a defiant joint communication declaring that they'd rather "die in these ditches" than give the place up.

Looks like the damn fools got their wish, he thought, quickly putting the sour notion out of his mind for now.

"One night right out of the blue Colonel Crocket showed up with some Tennessee boys. Maybe a dozen, I'm not sure. There was a fandango in his honor and most everybody was sleepin' it off the next mornin' when the lookout in the bell tower started ringin' the bell like it was the end of the world. Travis took a look and didn't see anything, but the lookout swore that he saw Mexican lancers out on the prairie. Buck sent two riders out and purty soon they came gallopin' back, hollerin' that the whole Mexican army was headed our way."

She stopped and licked her lips. Houston poured some water into a mug. She gulped it down and smiled sheepishly.

"Sorry, I didn't know I was so thirsty."

Houston smiled in return. "You're doin' just fine, Mrs. Dickinson. Take your time. Anything that is in my power to give you, you will have."

She gathered herself and the rest came out in one long desperate wail, as if she was trying to describe a nightmare.

"We grabbed what we could and ran into the Alamo just across the river. It took us all by surprise. Nobody had time to plan or think. We just took anything we could get our hands on."

The women and children – she and her baby were the only Anglos – were taken to a small room in the chapel, the strongest building in the crumbling old mission.

"I heard there was a parlay before the fightin' started but it didn't come to nuthin'. They demanded that we surrender and Travis answered with a cannon shot. The first few days the Mexicans rushed the walls once or twice but got turned back. Then our boys went out and burned those stick and mud shacks ... what do you call 'em?"

"*Jacales?*" responded Houston.

"That's it. Anyhow, they burned the ones closest to the walls so the Mexicans couldn't use 'em for cover." She stopped and took another long drink of water. "Travis sent out riders 'bout every day, askin' for help. They all expected you or Fannin over at Goliad to come."

For the first time, she looked like she might break down. "But you didn't. No one did 'cept thirty two boys from here in Gonzales. Where were you? Why didn't you come?"

To his surprise, Houston was embarrassed. He felt the

need to defend himself with an answer, for her sake, and for his own self-respect.

"Hockley!"

The aide poked his head into the tent.

"Sir?"

"How many men do we have?"

"Just a shade under four hundred; three hundred and seventy four, I believe."

"And how many of 'em are unfit for duty?"

"Forty seven as if this morning."

When Hockley resumed his place outside, Houston turned back to the pale and shaking widow.

"That's why we didn't come, Mrs. Dickinson. At the time, I was at Washington-on-the-Brazos and there were even fewer men here than there are now. Many of them were without arms. Still are, as it happens. We didn't even know what was happenin' until Travis' first messenger showed up, and that was several days into the siege. Even then, many of us couldn't believe that Santa Anna got here so soon and we resolved to wait a bit longer and create the nation we're fightin' for. I'm sorry, Mrs. Dickinson, and it truly grieves me to say it, but there was nothing we could do. If we lose this army, sad as it is, we lose Texas and then your husband's sacrifice will be for nothing."

"Would you have me approve?" she asked, her pride and defiant spirit boiling again.

"No, that would be too much to ask," Houston replied mildly. "But I would have you understand. Now, please go on. Where was Bowie in all this? When Juan Seguin showed up here, he said Jim was sick."

"He was dyin'," she said. "He had the typhoid. There was somethin' wrong with his lungs, too. The poor man could barely breathe. With that and the *vomito negro* he didn't have the strength to leave his bed. On the next to last day, I heard

9

that Colonel Crockett gave him a brace of pistols for when the Mexicans came. From what I saw ... after, he used them well before they took their vengeance on him."

"How many men did Santa Anna have?"

She shrugged. "I don't know. Thousands?"

"What happened at the end?"

She closed her eyes. Houston couldn't tell if she was gathering her memories or trying to force the awful images away.

"It was the thirteenth day, so early that it was still dark. It seemed like we'd been there forever. I went out to the well in the square to get some water for Angelina. Suddenly there was a lot of firin' and commotion at the north wall. I saw Travis run out of his room, headed to the wall with his shotgun in his hand. He hollered, "The Mexicans are upon us, boys. Give 'em hell." I ran back into the chapel to be with Angelina and the rest, so I didn't see anything else outside 'till it was over. The cannon fire shook the walls 'till I thought they might fall down and the cries of the men in the dark seemed to come from everywhere. The smoke burned my eyes 'till they teared. With all that and the wailin' of the women and children, I felt like I'd gone to hell."

The last time she saw her husband, he dashed down from his position at a cannon emplacement near the chapel.

"He hugged us close and cried, 'Good God, Sue! The Mexicans are inside the walls. If they spare you, save our child.' Then he ran back up to his cannon." She opened her eyes and lifted her chin in tribute to the man she loved. "They killed my husband there, but I'll wager they found no wounds in his back."

A few minutes later, a young man – "a boy, really" – named Galba Fuqua burst into the crowded little room. He desperately tried to tell her something, but he'd been shot through the jaw and couldn't speak well enough to be understood.

"All he could do was look at me with tears in his eyes before he ran back outside to die with the rest."

When the firing stopped, a Mexican officer entered the smoke-filled room and looked over the terrified women and children.

"He held out his hand, like this," she said, reaching out as if to help someone from the ground. "He said, 'If you want to save your life, come with me.'"

She saw Crockett's body in the open area just outside the chapel. "He was lyin' there as if he was only asleep, his broken rifle by his side."

The courteous officer took them to Santa Anna, who had just entered the compound. "They said he wanted to see the bodies of Travis, Bowie and Crockett. Someone took Angelina away, snatched her right out of my arms. I tried to take her back, but the officer who found me promised that they'd take care of her. He said that a child should not see the things that were done on that day. I don't know why, but I believed him when he said Angelina would be all right."

After pointing out Crockett's body, she led Santa Anna and several officers to the north wall. "Buck was shot in the head. He fell by one of the cannon. " She touched her forehead over one eye to indicate where he was hit. "It was just a day earlier that he gave Angelina his cat's eye ring. He put it on a string around her neck." She looked fondly at her child. "She's wearin' it now."

Then she led the group to Bowie's room near the gate at the south wall, stepping over two bodies as they entered.

"It looked like they hacked at him with bayonets. I said that I hoped he was dead by then and one of the officers said in English so I could understand it, 'A rebel deserves no mercy.'"

The next day, Santa Anna made such a bizarre offer that

the mother still seemed dazed by its audacity. Once he heard it, Houston couldn't blame her.

"He wanted to adopt Angelina. Can you imagine such a thing? He said that she would go to Mexico City and receive the finest education and care."

"Do you think he was serious?"

She shrugged. "He seemed awful smitten with her. I told him that I could not let the man who killed her father take my child. I said that I would kill myself if he tried. With so many dead already, it don't seem like much of a threat now, but it was the only thing I could think of."

The following day, she was given two dollars in silver, a blanket, and a mule and put out on the road with Travis' slave, Joe, which was where Smith found them.

Susanna Dickinson had no more to give. She was so exhausted that she could barely sit upright.

Houston rose to his feet, thanking her for her courage and her help. He explained that she could use his tent for as long as she wished, though he doubted that she heard him. She was asleep on the cot with her baby in her arms before the two men left the tent.

Outside, Houston found a lantern in the darkness and fumbled with it until he got a flame going.

"Got anything to add, Erastus?"

"Happened purty much like she said," he replied. "They put the bodies into piles and burned 'em. I don't think she knows that and I don't intend to tell her. She's been through enough. The officer who found her sounds like Juan Almonte. I knew him purty well before all this. He's a good man."

"Nobody got away?"

"Some tried, but there's no sign they made it."

"How bad was Santa Anna hurt?"

"Those boys gave good account of themselves, but he's got men to spare. If he's not already on the march he'll start soon, or send someone. Got another army under Urrea over to the east, probably headed for Goliad sooner or later, and patrols all over."

"How many men does he have altogether?'

"I'd say six thousand, give or take."

Smith reached inside his loose shirt and pulled out a formal looking document. He unfolded the thick parchment and handed it to Houston, still warm from the scout's body heat.

"Santa Anna gave her this, too. She don't have her letters and couldn't read it. Took me a while to get through all the flowery words."

"The General-in-Chief of the Army of Operations of the Mexican Republic, to the inhabitants of Texas:

Citizens! The causes which have conducted to this frontier a part of the Mexican Army are not unknown to you, a parcel of audacious adventurers, maliciously protected by some inhabitants of a neighboring republic dared to invade our territory, with the intention of dividing amongst themselves the fertile lands that are contained in the spacious Department of Texas; and even had the boldness to entertain the idea of reaching the capital of the republic. It became necessary to check and chastise such enormous daring; and in consequence, some exemplary punishments have already taken place in San Patricio, Lipantitlan and this city. I am pained to find amongst those adventurers the names of some colonists, to whom had been granted repeated benefits, and who had no motive of complaint against the government of their adopted country. These ungrateful men must also necessarily suffer the just punishment that the laws and the public vengeance demand. But if we are bound to punish the criminal, we are not the less compelled to protect the innocent. It is thus that the inhabitants of this country, let their origin be what it may, who should not appear to have been implicated in such iniquitous rebellion, shall be respected in their persons and property, provided they come forward and report themselves to the commander of the troops within eight days after they should have arrived in their respective settlements, in order to justify their conduct and to receive a document guaranteeing to them the right of enjoying that which lawfully belongs to them.

Bexarians! Return to your homes and dedicate yourselves to your domestic duties. Your city and the fortress of the Alamo are already in possession of the Mexican Army, composed of your own fellow citizens; and rest assured that no mass of foreigners will ever interrupt your repose, and much less, attack your lives and plunder your property. The Supreme Government has taken you under its protection and will seek for your good.

Inhabitants of Texas! I have related to you the orders that the army of operations I have the honor to command comes to execute; and therefore, the good will have nothing to fear. Fulfill always your duties as Mexican citizens, and you may expect the protection and benefit of the laws; and rest assured that you will never have reason to repent yourselves of having observed such conduct, for I pledge you in the name of the supreme authorities of the nation, and as your fellow citizen and friend, that what has promised you will be faithfully performed.

Antonio Lopez de Santa Anna

Houston folded the document in half and tucked it inside his waistcoat.

"This is in English," he said. "It's not aimed at the *Tejanos.* It's aimed at us. He's tryin' to scare us to death."

He put one big hand on Smith's shoulder. "Best not to mention this to anyone, at least not right away. We'll soon have panic enough as it is."

Smith gave Houston a questioning look.

"What are we goin' to do, General?'

"Erastus, my friend," Houston replied, "we are going to run like hell."

3

DESPITE HOUSTON WANTING to keep the news about the Alamo quiet for as long as possible, the wailing started almost immediately. The thirty two men of the Gonzales Mounted Ranger Company who rode to Bexar were all the men of fighting age the little town had to offer. It seemed as if everyone in Gonzales had lost a husband, a son, a father, or a brother. The desperate keening went on through the night as if it would never stop.

Hockley reported that several of the army's hot heads were talking about marching to Bexar to take on Santa Anna's thousands.

Houston could only sneer at such stupidity. "We have probably a hundred men who don't even have arms. What do they intend to do? Walk into Santa Anna's camp, punch *El Presidente* in the nose, and demand that he surrender?"

Not expecting an answer, Houston considered the men crowded into his tent, taking comfort in the fact that these were men he could count on, the best he had.

In addition to Hockley and Smith, he'd called in Juan Seguin and Henry Karnes. Seguin came from one of the old

Tejano families, Mexicans born or raised in Texas. As young as he was, he had already served as Bexar's *alcade*, as did his father, Don Erasmo, before him. The liberal Seguins detested the autocratic Santa Anna and whole-heartedly supported the revolution. Seguin was one of the last messengers Travis sent out of the Alamo, getting away on the fastest mount that the ill-fated mission had to offer. The handsome, well-educated Seguin spoke English better than most of the Americans in camp.

Karnes was different breed, a rough-and-tumble Tennessean who'd come to Texas to make his fortune like so many others. Although probably twenty five years younger than Smith, who was pushing fifty, the stocky, red-haired Karnes had wisdom and skill beyond his age, and was very nearly Smith's equal already.

"What happened to Mrs. Dickinson and the babe?" Smith asked.

""She slept like the dead for abut an hour, woke up and announced that she'd rather sleep outside," answered Houston. "She'd spent too long cooped up in that room at the Alamo and couldn't bear it any more."

With that, he got down to business.

"We'll be pullin' out of here soon, two hours at most. Erastus and Henry, you and your scouts will be our eyes and ears. I want to know what every Mexican with Santa Anna is up to and I want to know what they're *goin'* to do as soon as they know it. Cast a wide net and report as often as you can. Remember, there's no such thing as too much information, as long as it's *accurate* information."

He turned to Seguin. "Juan, you and your *Tejanos* ... how many do you have now?"

"Twenty six, all mounted."

"You will be the rear guard. Goose the stragglers along and watch over those poor people from Gonzales as best you can before they scatter to the wind as they no doubt will. When Santa Anna sends out patrols, I need you to keep 'em off our back so that our numbers and where we're headed remains a mystery, as much as possible. I want no surprises, not even good ones. And despite all the bluster about wantin' to fight, I have no doubt there will be deserters. Let 'em go. "

"After what they heard about Bear, I reckon we've already lost twenty five, or so, already," Smith said.

Houston made a dismissive gesture. "I might have to make an example out of one or two eventually, but for now I'd rather have the faint hearts out of here. Others are on the way and we'll gain numbers as we travel. I ordered Fannin to retreat from the *presidio* at Goliad and join us with his four hundred. We will *not* win this fight from behind walls."

"General, about these people ..."

Houston knew where Seguin was headed and stopped him before he could finish.

"I know. Juan. It's sad, but there's not much we can do for 'em, except to send them away from us so they won't get caught in any more unpleasantness."

A thought occurred to Houston. "How many wagons do we have?"

"Four," answered Karnes.

"Give 'em three. That should help a little. At least they won't have to carry everything on their backs. We'll keep one wagon to haul our ammunition and powder. Dismantle our two cannon and throw 'em in the Guadalupe. The damn things would only slow us down. The roads are too muddy. "

The general motioned toward a small wooden box underneath his cot. "Dig into that box. That's the army treasury, all three hundred dollars of it. Distribute that amongst 'em, too."

"All of it?" asked Karnes.

"All of it," replied Houston.

"It ain't much," observed Smith.

"You could say that about the whole army," Houston said. "We ain't much, but we're all we've got. I'm surprised Santa Anna isn't after us already. We're only fifty miles from Bexar."

"I hear he's sendin' Sesma after us, and El President will be along directly," Smith said. "Just now, Santa Anna's expendin' all his energy in the marriage bed."

Seeing the dumbfounded looks on the other men, Smith explained that it was one of Santa Anna's habits to pick out the prettiest young woman in a town, woo her with all the pomp and personality he possessed – and even his critics admitted that he had plenty of both – and "marry" her in a false ceremony where he had one of his smooth aides pose as a priest. He then enjoyed the benefits of "marriage" for several days before moving on.

"Her name's Barrera, Mechora Barrera. I know the family a little. She's a purty little thing."

"That works?" asked Karnes.

"Seems to," Smith said. "When he's finished, he has 'em shipped off to Mexico City, or his place in San Luis Potosi, all real proper. Don't know what happens to 'em there. I wonder what his real wife thinks?"

"Damn, I never thought of that," laughed Karnes, who was known to cut a wide swath through what few single women there were in Texas.

"Well maybe that's because you ain't the Napoleon of the West," Smith said, poking fun at his young friend.

"The what?" asked Karnes.

"That's what he calls himself," interrupted Houston, not sure that Karnes knew who Napoleon was, and more than a little surprised that Smith did.

On that mercifully light note, the men started to leave, but Houston held them back with a gesture.

"Juan, Erastus and Henry, there's one more thing. Once we're safely away, I want the town burned so that there will be no shelter for the enemy. Anything we can't carry - supplies, provisions, and tents, including this one - all gets burned, too. See to it."

As they filed out of the tent, Houston gave Hockley a look indicating that the aide should hang back.

Once they were alone, he explained, "Hockley, in addition to your regular duties, I'm going to assign you one more task."

"Yes, sir," the aide responded eagerly. "Whatever you need."

Houston shook his head. "Don't be so quick to agree. This may be the most difficult thing I'll ever ask of you. And it's not an order, it's a request. Refuse it, and I will not think less of you."

Houston plunged ahead before his own reluctance got in the way. He never liked confessing to weakness, even though he knew that he possessed many, but that was what he was about to do.

"You are to keep me from drinking. During the course of this campaign, however long it takes, I must not touch spirits of any kind. I have no doubt that the pressure both military and political will be immense and it is vital that I keep my wits about me. I am all too aware of my richly deserved reputation as a drunkard and my enemies must have no excuse to pillory me with it, not that my sobriety will stop them. But it must be known that I am sober and for that to happen sober I must be."

"If you see me start to drink, stop me. If you sense that I want to drink, talk me out of it. Remind me of this conversation. If you see me searching for liquor, hide it from me and make sure I don't find it. No matter what I say, no matter what names I call you, no matter how much I threaten you, I must not drink. Not one drop. And all of it must be done as quietly as possible."

Houston paused to let the unusual words sink in, giving the young officer a chance to refuse.

"Do you understand how important this is? There is no one I trust more than you, which is why I ask you to do this. There is no glory in it and it will not get your name written in the pages of history. But you will have my undying gratitude."

"I can do it, General," Hockley replied. "And I will."

"Son, you had better."

Hockley left the tent visibly strutting with pride abut how much "his" general trusted him.

Young men, Huston laughed into his chest as he sank down on his stool. If they only knew how much they didn't know.

He lifted his head when Seguin re-entered the tent. It was obvious that he'd been waiting outside.

"Did you hear all that?"

"Yes. I didn't mean to, but I did."

"You weren't supposed to. You have your orders. Why were you lurking out there?" asked Houston with more asperity that he felt. He knew why Seguin needed time alone with him and was prepared to deal with it; his first crises of command.

"It's about our orders," Seguin explained. "General, whatever we report, we need to know that you will believe us. Because if you don't, my men will wonder why we are here at all."

It was as Houston thought, something he knew that he would have to deal with sooner or later, although he would have preferred later.

"Sit down and talk, Juan," he said, motioning toward the cot that lately seemed to be used for everything but sleep.

Seguin indicated that he preferred to stand, although he did toss his sombrero on the cot.

"General, my men are as good as any you have. But we don't feel like we are part of this army, that we are wanted here. And then we wonder why we are fighting."

Houston pulled a half-smoked cheroot from his waistcoat pocket and lit up, content to let Seguin have his say. The man had earned it ten times over.

"There was no reason for us to be surprised at Bexar. Two days before, one of my scouts reported that Santa Anna's advance guard was closing in, but no one believed him. After all, he was *only* a Mexican. Then two men of my company, Andrew Barcena and Anselmo Bergerra, rode in here with the report that the Alamo had fallen. But what did you do? You put them under guard and denounced them as spies sent to spread false information. You didn't believe it until Deaf brought in the Anglo woman and her baby. Was that also because my men are *only* Mexicans?"

"We risk more than any of you. If we lose, you can go back to the United States. *This* is our home." Seguin stamped his foot on the ground in frustration. "We have no where else to go. But what does it matter? After all, we are *only* Mexicans."

Houston took his time before answering; drawing mightily on the cigar, so close to finished that it burned his fingers. Decent tobacco was in short supply, but maybe smoking more could make up for sobriety? He didn't have high hopes for that theory.

"Juan, I can't tell you what was in the hearts and minds of the boys at the Alamo. They shouldn't have been there anyhow. I sent Bowie with orders to save what weapons and powder he could, blow up the place, and get out. As to your men here, I had to be sure. I needed better and more information. Until then, I had to keep it quiet to avoid panic. This so-called army would have evaporated otherwise. I didn't have proper hold of 'em yet. Still don't. Half of the men would have marched to the Alamo to be slaughtered and the other half likely would have deserted. Most of the brave talk is just wind. We're in a delicate condition just now. Mrs. Dickinson wasn't credible because she's an Anglo. She was credible because she was *there*. Her's was no second-hand report. She *saw* it happen."

Houston ground the cigar out beneath his boot.

"I owe your men an apology. Would you send a messenger and have them report to me ... no, ask them if they would be so kind to meet with me at their earliest convenience."

Houston grinned. He could tell by the look on Seguin's face that he had defused the crisis for now, although he knew that it would rise again. Too many men in this army either thought that every Mexican was an enemy, or that they were little better than niggers. Seguin and his *Tejanos* showed extraordinary patience every day. In their place, Houston doubted that he could do the same.

"But only as long as their earliest convenience is within the next ninety minutes, or so," he added, "which is just about how much longer we'll be in Gonzales."

4

GONZALES WAS BURNING.

Intent on getting the army the ten miles to Peach Creek by dawn, Houston didn't bother to look back until they were more than three miles out of town.

"General, you might want to see this," suggested Hockley.

Houston impatiently jerked the reins and wheeled his horse to take a look at what had caught his aide's attention. It was a remarkable sight. Even from miles away, he could see flames from the burning town lick at the night. Scattered explosions sent showers of sparks high into the black sky, caused by small barrels of gunpowder that the army either had no place for, or was of such poor quality that they weren't worth carrying.

Gonzales wasn't much, but it was home to more than a few men, women and children. Lovers met there. They married there. They raised families there. And they died there. Now those same families, many of them mourning their men killed at the Alamo, plodded across the dark prairie, suddenly cut adrift in the world. Most were on foot, with a fortunate few, usually the very young or the very old, riding in ox carts, while their lives burned on the horizon.

Over the last few hours, Houston had heard so many sad tales he didn't think that he could bear anymore and hardened his heart to them all. To his right, Houston saw a man he'd known for years. Even in the weak moonlight, he could see tears glistening on Henry Eggleston's weathered face as he watched the flames consume his home and storehouse. He'd just received three thousand dollars worth of merchandise a few days earlier, ordered months ago. His small herd of seventeen cattle were scattered across the prairie. Without a home, business, or livestock, like so many others the suddenly impoverished Eggleston had no where to go, a refugee in a dark and brutal world.

Ironically, Gonzales was where the revolution started, a dispute over a little six-pound cannon the Mexican army loaned the town to protect itself from Indians, although Houston never understood what a cannon was supposed to accomplish against the hard-riding Comanche.

When tension between Mexico and the Texian settlers began to boil, the army demanded that the cannon be returned, but the settlers refused to give it up. In what sounded to Houston like more comedy than drama, the settlers buried the cannon in an effort to hide it. When it occurred to them that nothing was more worthless than a buried cannon, they dug it up and loaded it with scrap metal, all ready to fire. Someone made a banner featuring a silhouette of the cannon and the defiant words, "Come And Take It!"

When the settlers actually fired the cannon, the handful of Mexican army regulars from the local garrison wisely retreated. The only Texian casualty came when one of the settlers fell off his horse and bloodied his nose.

As ridiculous as it seemed, after that there was no turning back. The revolution had broken wide open.

And now, here they were, desperate and on the run.

5

THE RIDER GALLOPED in from Washington-on-the-Brazos, his horse lathered and blowing hard and his saddlebag stuffed full of documents.

Sitting on his saddle in the middle of the muddy field where the army camped for the night, by the flickering light of a lantern Houston assessed the information the rider brought. His tent went up in flames back in Gonzales, along with most of the rest of the army's baggage, and he missed it. It was a cold damp night and Houston pulled his buckskin coat tighter around his body, full of regret that he couldn't warm himself with a dram or two of whiskey.

"Well, well, well, it looks as if finally we have ourselves a government," he said, speaking quietly to himself since, by his order, there was no one within hearing. He wanted to assess the information privately before making a general announcement. True, it was only a provisional government, to exist until the revolution was won or they were all killed or driven out of Texas, but for now it was all the government Texas had.

President David Gourveneur Burnet ... the words just didn't seem natural, not when applied to that dour, overbearing blowhard. How in the hell did that man ever become president? When Houston rode out of Washington to take command of the army at Gonzales, Burnet wasn't even a proper delegate to the convention, yet he somehow managed to weasel his way to the presidency.

Looking at it with the experienced eye of a former governor and congressman, Houston saw how could happen. The two most likely candidates for president – himself and Stephen Austin – were both absent. The sickly Austin was back in the United States raising money, arms, and men, supposedly having a fair amount of success, too. Their absence left an opening for someone like Burnet, who, in Houston's opinion, talked better than he accomplished, but sometimes in politics that was enough to take a man far.

A stocky little plug of a man with bushy-brown whiskers, Burnet had a habit of carrying a Bible in one pocket and a loaded pistol in the other. He strongly disapproved of liquor and profanity, which in Houston's opinion made him a man of dubious character right there. In their many personal and political disagreements, Houston had taken to calling the little man *"Wetumpka,"* which he told everyone was Cherokee for "hog thief." As far as Houston knew, Burnet had never stolen a hog in his life, and the word actually meant something like "rumbling waters" in the Creek language, but he loved seeing Burnet turn red-faced and wave his arms in he air as he fulminated about the nickname.

Smiling at the memory of Burnet's displeasure, Houston moved on down the list. The convention made a good choice by making Lorenzo de Zavala vice president. Without the *Tejanos* the revolution would almost certainly fail and at least one of them had to be named to high office. The courtly De Zavala was one of the founders of the Mexican republic when it declared its independence from Spain 15 years ago. At considerable personal risk, he broke away from Santa Anna when the Mexican president renounced the nation's liberal constitution of 1824, which included the ease of immigration into Texas. de Zavala was married to a New Orleans woman and had a sizable plantation near the San Jacinto River. If the new republic was lucky, his polish and experience could moderate some of Burnet's aggressive stupidity.

Naming Robert Potter Secretary of the Navy wasn't a good sign. One of Burnet's few close friends, he served for a brief time in the United States Navy, which he assumed gave him all the experience necessary to command the three little ships that made up the Texas Navy. But at a time when the revolution needed steady hands and cool thinkers, Potter was anything but, a man too easily ruled by his own passions. Back in North Carolina, he was thrown in jail for castrating two men who had their way with his wife, although it was common knowledge that the way they had was mostly his wife's idea. Not much later, he was tossed out of the North Carolina legislature for cheating at cards. It was one thing to cheat at cards, Houston laughed to himself, but being bad at it was even worse.

Houston went on down the list, approving of some appointments and grumbling about others: Bailey Hardeman as Secretary of the Treasury; Attorney General David Thomas; Secretary of State Sam Carson ... he knew some well and others just barely. Some were good choices, others were terrible.

He perked up when he saw that Tom Rusk was the Secretary of War. Now there was a man he could work with, which was a good thing because Houston would report directly to Rusk. True, he was a protégé of that starchy South Carolina swine John Calhoun, the deadly enemy of Houston's own mentor, Andrew Jackson, now serving the last year of his two terms as President. Some twenty years ago, Calhoun threatened to have a young Sam Houston cashiered out of the army for no good reason, but Houston had always found Rusk to be a man with an open mind and a good heart. Unlike too many others from the South, where the silly notions of honor all too often led to pistols at dawn over so-called insults no one could quite remember, you could disagree with the new Secretary of War, argue until dawn, and not be challenged to a duel later that day. Houston felt sure than he had an ally in Tom Rusk.

Rummaging through the rest of the papers, Houston discovered a proclamation from the "Executive Department" of the government of Texas. He chuckled at the pomposity that could only have come from Burnet, who called on "to the People in Eastern Texas" to join the cause.

"Gen. Houston is at his post on the frontier with eight hundred men and reinforcements constantly arriving," Burnet wrote. "Our army is in high spirits and full of confidence."

Houston summoned a nearby private. "Post this on a tree in the middle of camp where everyone can see it. The men deserve to know about their new government."

They were good words and the men would like them, although Houston had the uneasy feeling that his relations with Burnet would never be better than they were right now.

And eight hundred men? Where in the world did the President get that figure? It took a moment before Houston realized that it was his own fault. He'd exaggerated the army's numbers to put some heart into the men as they trudged through the miserable rain and mud on their way to the Colorado River and it must have gotten back to Burnet, who took it as gospel. Well, reinforcements *were* coming in every day and the desertions had practically stopped, too. They'd for sure have more than eight hundred men when Fannin's four hundred were added, probably closer to a thousand.

But where *was* Fannin? Why hadn't anyone heard from him?

"HE'S STILL THERE?" Houston couldn't believe it. "He hasn't moved an inch."

"He did move a bit, he just didn't go anywhere," Smith replied, removing his sweat-stained hat while they walked along a creek upstream from the camp. "It's almost funny, what that man did."

Houston didn't see the humor, but then he was the one who carried the responsibility. Sometimes he envied Smith for his independence. He'd just ridden into camp from a long-range scout that included a look at Colonel James Fannin and his men in Goliad.

Houston still wore his long-fringed buckskin coat to keep out the chill. His boots with the fancy brass spurs shaped as eagles sank into the mud with every step. By contrast, Smith seemed move so lightly across the ground in his moccasins that he left no impression he was ever there.

According to the canny scout, Fannin did set out to relieve the Alamo a few days before Houston arrived in Gonzales, but he dawdled for so long that it was late in the day before he got started. After not even than two miles, a wagon broke down. By the time it was repaired, it was near dark and Fannin decided that the men might as well stay where they were for the night, with Goliad still practically in sight.

For some reason, Fannin seemed to change his mind overnight. After an inconclusive officers' conference the next morning, the colonel decided to march back to Goliad, where he sent out a letter of explanation extolling his brilliant "retrograde" movement.

"General, what does ret-ro-grade mean?" asked Smith, carefully sounding out each syllable.

"It means you start to do something, stop, and go back to where you started." Fannin had orders to destroy the *presidio* and fall back to join the main army. Instead, he fiddled and dallied back and forth like a delicate maiden who couldn't decide between suitors and needed a serious dose of smelling salts. "In Fannin's case, it means you don't know what in hell you're doing."

"Well, it sure sounds plenty ret-ro-grade to me," mused Smith. "I did hear that he intended to start out again, but decided to stay put when the Alamo fell."

"Erastus, how old is this information?"

""A few days older'n I'd like. Took me a while to get back here. Mexicans got patrols all over."

"So Fannin could be on the move by now?"

"Sure, he could, but I don't think so. He's got some patrols out roundin' up the settlers that are in Urrea's path and don't want to leave 'till they get back to Goliad. What he don't know is that some of 'em already been captured or killed, probably most of 'em. I'm 'fraid Fannin's sittin' there waitin' for men who ain't never comin' back."

6

"MOTHER AND FATHER,"

"I do not know when this letter will reach you, or if it will ever reach you, but I wanted to take a few minutes before the fires are dimmed in camp to tell you something of my adventures here."

"As you may have already heard, we are now a nation. The fifty nine delegates to the Texas Constitutional Convention formed a new government at a forlorn and dismal little place called Washington-on-the-Brazos. The town consists of no more than a dozen wretched cabins or shanties laid out in the woods. There is not one decent house in it, and only one defined street, with the stumps still standing in the mud. I happened to travel there from Nacogdoches because I heard about the convention and didn't know where else to go to serve in the fight for independence from Mexico. I am afraid that reliable information is rare in Texas at this time."

"I arrived in Washington-on-the-Brazos on April 30, the day before the convention met in a meeting room that was so new its boards still oozed sap. Indeed, one might accurately call it unfinished as it was without doors or window glass. Cotton cloth was stretched across the open windows, which at least partially excluded the cold wind. The delegates spend a day and night drafting a Declaration of

Independence, which was largely written by George Childress of Tennessee. The essence of it can be found in these words: 'When a government has ceased to protect the lives, liberty, and property of the people, and when that government has become a military dictatorship, it becomes the right of the people to abolish such a government and create another to secure their future welfare and happiness. The Mexican nation has allowed General Santa Anna to overturn the constitution of this country. He now offers us the cruel choice of either abandoning our homes or submitting to his tyranny ... We do hereby resolve and declare that our political connection with the Mexican nation has forever ended; and that the people of Texas do now constitute a free and independent people.'"

"Then, on the evening of March 2, a dispatch from William Barret Travis arrived at the convention, to the consternation of everyone in attendance. Travis, who seemed well known to virtually one and all here, reported a skirmish with Mexican troops let by Mexican President Antonio Lopez de Santa Anna at a fortress called the Alamo in San Antonio de Bejar, where Travis commanded, and where more Mexican troops arrived every day."

"Amidst all the furor, we were all much relieved to learn that Colonel James Fannin was reported to be on the march from Goliad to the Alamo with more than 350 men, so it was believed that Travis and his garrison was safe, at least for some time, so the convention could begin to establish a government."

"The declaration was unanimously approved and signed by all members. A committee immediately set to work to draft a constitution to provide for an interim government to serve until the Republic of Texas is born, when there is to be a popularly elected president and vice president, a congress composed of a senate and a house of representatives, and a supreme court. In short, it will be a mirror of the United States government."

"But suddenly there came a time when it seemed as if there would be no one remaining at Washington-on-the-Brazos to shape a government. On March 6, another dispatch was received from

Travis, dated March 3. *All the members of the convention and hangers-on such as myself crowded into the meeting room to hear it read: 'We have contended for ten days against an enemy whose numbers are variously estimated from fifteen hundred to six thousand men. I hope your honorable body will hasten on reinforcements, ammunitions and provisions to our aid so soon as possible.'*

"'God and Texas – Victory or Death'"

"We subsequently learned that Fannin did not march to the relief of the Alamo after all. While we did not know it then, by the time we received his message the gallant Travis and his men were already dead. As I'm sure you can understand, the cry for help stirred the convention into great excitement. A motion was put forward to 'immediately adjourn, arm and march to the relief of the Alamo.' A great many persons prepared to do just that, with or without the approval of the convention."

"But one mighty voice rose in dissent and that voice soon carried the day. With his deep and compelling tones, army commander-in-chief Sam Houston, late of Tennessee, dominated the convention with his persuasive argument that it was of the utmost importance to remain at work. In the meantime, he declared that he would go to Gonzales and rally the Texas forces to stand against Santa Anna and his thousands and relieve the men besieged at the Alamo."

"I must say that Houston created more sensation than any man I have met during my three months in Texas and perhaps even in my entire life. He appears to be in his early 40s. While somewhat worn in appearance, he possesses great presence and a robust military manner, typically carrying a pistol at his belt and a sword at his side. As I understand it, he sometimes struggles with drink and the tales of his prodigious bouts with the demon are legendary, as are the tales of his colorful background, from his bravery and wounds during the Creek Indian War, to his rise to governor of Tennessee and his rapid fall as a result of marital difficulties, followed by his years in the wilderness living with the Cherokee, and his resurrection after thrashing a Ohio congressman on the streets of Washing-

ton. *I should report that he does have many enemies here, including some good and reasonable men, who claim that he is nothing more than a monument to ambition and vanity, a vainglorious man to whom treachery and nefarious plots are as natural as breathing. A man, in short, who is not to be trusted under any circumstances."*

"Despite some grumbling from a few of the delegates, Houston gained the support of the convention and soon galloped out of town, accompanied by his aide, Colonel George Washington Hockley, and three volunteers, including, you may be surprise to learn, your own son. I admit that I have become devoted to the man, while still recognizing that he possesses the weaknesses and inconsistencies that all men possess. I do believe that he is Texas' great hope."

"A peculiar thing happened after only a few miles on the road. The general called a halt, dismounted, knelt, and pressed an ear to the ground. A trick he claimed to have learned from his years with the Cherokee. If there still was cannon fire at the Alamo, he said that he would somehow detect the vibrations. After a few minutes listening, he rose to his feet and gravely told us that he feared the cannon had fallen silent. Full of apprehension, our party rode on to Gonzales, a journey of several days."

"As much as I admire the general, I after some reflection I have come to the conclusion that the great man lied. There is no other way to put it. San Antonio de Bejar was, after all, some 150 miles away. I do not believe that even the keenest sense could detect any vibration or sound at that distance. Instead, it is my belief that it was all a charade and he never intended to go to the aid of the Alamo. We have too few men and our forces are too scattered and untrained to take such action. At the convention, he said what people needed to hear and wanted to believe in order to achieve a larger goal. If that makes him duplicitous – and it most certainly does – then so be it. History will judge us all right or wrong and I believe him to be right, at least thus far."

"We later discovered that the Alamo had fallen even before we left Washington-on-the-Brazos and that Gonzales was in immediate

danger. A detachment of some 700 Mexican troops under an able general named Siezman, or Sesma, or Seezma (these foreign names do confound me!) was on the way, with numbers twice our own, we were told."

"And so, after burning poor Gonzales to the ground, we began a miserable retreat east through the mud and rain that greatly impeded our movements. There was grumbling from many, if not most, of the men, including several newcomers, including one in particular, Sidney Sherman. A Kentucky manufacturer of cotton bagging, Sherman sold his plant there and raised a volunteer company to help liberate Texas. He is one of our most influential hotspurs and seems eager to take on the entire Mexican army with his company alone. Although he has never, as far as I know, been in a military engagement of any kind, he certainly looks the part of a dashing officer, typically wearing a dark blue coat trimmed with silver lace and a handsome dress sword at his side. He constantly criticizes General Houston, but stops just short of accusing him of cowardice. Alas, he is by no means alone in his sentiments. Of the many men who claim to be spoiling for a fight, if a fight were to come I do not believe they would be as spoiling as they think they are, although the rhetoric is heated at times. For myself, I know that I will fight when necessary, although I do not look forward to it."

"While General Houston certainly does not confide in me - or anyone at all, if the camp gossip is true - it is easy enough to read a map and deduce his aims. Despite what he said at the convention, I believe that he always intended to retreat from the thinly settled Gonzales area, where the army was poorly supplied, and retreat until we at least crossed the Colorado River at Burnham's Crossing. There, we will be closer to the most populous area of Texas, where supplies and reinforcements should be plentiful. The swollen river will also form a temporary barrier against the heavily equipped Mexican troops and it will take some time for them to cross. Our strategy of retreat will also get us into the more heavily wooded country of east Texas, where the effectiveness of the Mexican cavalry – I have never seen such horsemen and understand that their long lances are remarkably effective – will be much reduced."

"The general drives us at an unrelenting pace. What is remarkable to me is that with the way he has of constantly riding up and down and back and forth across our lines, he must cover at least three times more distance than the rest of the army. With the stress of command, his temper is fierce and he seems to be always raging against something or someone. Unfortunately he has alienated more than a few of our men with his unrelenting fulminations."

"As grim as our march has been, it is not without humor. I must tell you a tale. Noah Smithwick, a young blacksmith, was with a group of scouts north of our column when they awoke one morning to find a full division of Mexicans under a general named Gaona, or Genoa - blast these names! – camped on the other side of a small river. Our scouts moved out so hurriedly that they forgot about the guard they posted at another nearby crossing, an old man known as 'Uncle Jimmy' Curtis, who, being well into his 60s, may be the oldest man in the army and by reputation one of the most formidable tipplers in Texas. He certainly is one of the feistiest. He lost a son-in-law named Washington Cottle at the Alamo and frequently announces that he intends to avenge him by killing at least five Mexicans."

"As Smithwick, a young man of parts I have become close to during our retreat, tells the story, he found 'Uncle Jimmy' sitting against a tree, with a bottle of whiskey beside him, as unconscious of danger as a lizard sunning himself on a rock."

"Smithwick cried, 'Mount up and ride for your life, old man. The Mexicans are on the other side of the river and our men are all gone.'"

"'The hell they are,'" replied Uncle Jimmy, exhibiting the great calm often induced by alcohol. 'Light and take a drink with me.'"

"'This is no time for drinking," Smithwick replied in desperation. "They might be here any minute.'"

"'Well, let's drink to their confusion,' persisted Uncle Jimmy."

"*Seeing that the old man would not move until he drank with him, Smithwick nervously dismounted and accepted a dram or two before they finally struck out, with the Mexican division in sight.*"

"*According to my friend, Uncle Jimmy was not in the least disturbed by his close call, declaring, 'At least we can say that no damn Mexican scared us away.'*"

"*I must close now. It is time for lights out in camp. Rest assured that I am well and happy. I know that our cause is just and I am confident of our ultimate success. I am certain as ever that one day I will make my fortune here, a land like no other.*"

"*Your devoted son,*"

"*Matthew*"

7

As the army slogged east, picking up recruits mile after mile just as Houston hoped, he regretted his pledge not to drink. Tending toward the prickly and profane at the best of times, the unfortunate combination of abstinence and the obstinate nature of his men threatened to drive him mad. A herd of jackasses would be easier to command.

Memories of the trouble that General Jackson had with his undisciplined militia during the Creek War did nothing to brighten Houston's mood. More than 20 years ago, he watched in awe as Jackson brought his rebellious army to heel and turned it into a lethal war machine. Houston wanted to do the same thing – he *had* to do the same thing - but there were too many times when frustration and temper got the best of him.

Strangely enough, thoughts about controlling his temper only made his temper worse. As he rode up and down the line urging the weary men forward, he fumed that he was leading a mob, not an army. There was nothing remotely military about it. Its shabby appearance reflected its nature. Some men wore buckskin, others wore cloth, most of it homespun and ragged, while most were dressed in a mix of both. There weren't many boots to be seen, mostly battered shoes, worn moccasins, and more than a few bare feet. Headwear included broad-brimmed sombreros, a handful of military caps, beaver hats, top hats, a few coonskin caps with the tail hanging down behind, straw hats that looked like rats had dined on them, and sometimes no hats at all. Buffalo robes were favored to keep the rain off because blankets soaked through too easily, but there weren't enough buffalo robes for everyone. Instead of canteens for drinking water, most of the' men carried Mexican gourds. Weapons included everything from long rifles and muskets to pistols, Bowie knives, axes, and swords. One San Felipe blacksmith who joined the army after his brother was killed carried two nine-pound hammers as weapons.

Despite the drills Houston insisted on twice a day just after sunrise and just before sunset, most of the men still wouldn't know a military command if it was tattooed on their noses. Even if they understood it, more than likely they do what they pleased anyway. As militia, which most of them were, they expected to march and fight when and where they chose, and then disband when and where they chose. To fight a war to be free from taking orders from Mexico City, but to have to take orders to do it was beyond their comprehension. They knew nothing of drill and maneuver and strategic considerations flew over their heads like birds. Not understanding the difference between popularity and leadership, they expected to elect their company officers and then bitterly complained when Houston did not allow it.

The general's thoughts were interrupted when he realized that the line wasn't moving.

"Why the hell have we stopped?" The blank looks all around him revealed that no one knew the answer.

Spurring his horse to the front of the line, Houston saw a

private named Rhodes standing knee-deep in the middle of Rocky Creek, where he'd stopped to take a drink, fill his water gourd, and clean off his muddy shoes, stalling the long line of men and animals behind him.

The raging Houston galloped into the creek, came up behind the unsuspecting private, seized him by the back of his collar, and galloped out of the creek on the other side, with Rhodes dangling at the side of his horse, the private's feet frantically scrambling for purchase on the ground. Ignoring Rhodes' wails, Houston kept going until he found a thicket full of thorns and threw his helpless victim into the middle of it, bellowing "God damn your worthless soul" as he did.

But even as he wheeled his horse around and motioned the men forward, Houston knew that he'd made a mistake. Rhodes wasn't much of a soldier. A few nights earlier, he was reprimanded for falling asleep on guard duty. But however satisfying it was to throw the man around like a sack of potatoes, the humiliation would almost certainly turn Rhodes into a martyr for the army's malcontents. If a private needed to be disciplined then his immediate superior was the man for the job, not the general.

After brooding about it all through the rest of the day, late that night as was his habit Houston wandered out of camp alone, taking a look at the ground ahead for the best route.

An hour later, on foot as he led his horse back into camp, the distracted general was challenged by a sentry, who cried, "Halt!" as he popped out from behind a tree, rifle at the ready.

"You damn fool, I'm General Houston. I can go anywhere I want anytime I want."

He could see that the young sentry wasn't happy about what he was doing, which didn't stop him from doing it.

"I'm real sorry, but my orders say that no one passes in or out without written permission. You look like the general, sure 'nuff. But I've never seen him up close and that don't change my orders anyhow, whoever you might be ... uh, sir."

Houston was seized by a fit of uncontrollable laughter that was so strong he didn't have the strength to remain standing and had to sink down on a stump before he fell down. The unexpected response only made the sentry take a tighter grip on his long rifle, convinced that he had a mad man on his hands.

"Well, my friend, if those are your orders then you'd best obey them," Houston said, wiping the tears from his eyes. He couldn't remember the last time he had a laugh like this. "If you'd kindly send word to the officer of the day I think we can clear this whole thing up."

Three minutes later, the officer appeared. Once he learned what happened, the appalled officer began berating the sentry as they stood nose to nose in the darkness.

Houston stopped him with a big hand on his shoulder. "Lieutenant, it seems to me that this sentry is one of the few men in this army who knows what the hell he's doing. It's my opinion that he deserves praise, not criticism."

Still smiling, Houston led his horse past the two confused men, headed into camp. A sudden thought made him turn on his heel.

"More than that, I'd say he deserves a reward." He looked at the sentry. "You're a private, aren't you?"

The sentry nodded, not nearly as sure of himself as he was a few minutes ago.

"Well, you're now a corporal. Find me in the mornin' and I'll see that you get your papers."

Now *that* was more like it, Houston thought as he walked into camp. Still, he had to do better. Maybe it would help if he stopped asking himself what Andrew Jackson would do and come up with his own solutions. It was about time.

8

SOME PEOPLE TAKE DAYS, or even weeks, to make a bad impression. Sidney Sherman managed to alienate almost everyone in just a few minutes. It was a remarkable performance.

"If you ask me, my boys in the Kentucky Rifles can lick the Mexicans ten to one all by ourselves, if need be." Sherman waved in the direction of Beeson's Crossing not far from camp on the Colorado River, about twenty miles north of where the army crossed the river a few days ago. "Makes me wonder what you all been waitin' for. I hear Sesma's numbers across the river are about the same as ours. Are we here to fight or are we here to run? Answer me that. Seems to me we'll never have a better chance."

Although the other officers looked to Houston for the answer, he let the question die in the air. Sherman wasn't interested in an answer anyway. The brash Kentuckian didn't realize that he'd just insulted every man in the army who wasn't one of his, even those who agreed with him. It was best to let him dangle on his own rope for a while.

The officers' meeting, like most such meetings, hadn't accomplished anything, which was why Houston rarely called them. Sesma's 1,200 men were on one side of the swollen river, facing Houston's 1,100, but neither army was willing to make the first move, mostly because there wasn't a good move to make. With all of its baggage, cannon, and heavy equipment, for the time being the river was impassable for the Mexicans. For his part, Houston refused to order his undisciplined army to cross a flooded river under the guns of an experienced, war-hardened enemy armed with at least two cannon. If the river fell, an attack of some kind might be possible, especially if Fannin was finally on the move and his men could somehow be maneuvered so that Sesma was caught between the two Texian forces, not that Houston had particularly high hopes when it came to Jim Fannin moving anywhere.

Another consideration was that a Mexican courier captured by Henry Karnes revealed that another Mexican army led by Antonio Ganoa had already occupied Bastrop and had orders to follow the Old San Antonio Road all the way to Nacogdoches, deep in the heart of the piney woods country. At the same time, Urrea was moving up along the coast from the south, picking off town after town like ripe plums. After capturing every port but Galveston, he had to be closing in on Goliad by now. Santa Anna was on the march out of Bejar, too. The Mexicans certainly weren't short of generals.

Houston held these meetings from time to time to gauge the mood of his officers. It was good for him to see how they rubbed up against each other, with alliances, likes, dislikes, feuds, and friendships seeming to shift almost every day.

Even Houston admitted that Sidney Sherman looked the part of a fighting officer, with his glistening sword, blue jacket with silver trim, and polished riding boots. He was not a big man, but held himself erect so that he appeared taller than he was, one of those men who seemed to strut even while sitting down. How Sherman kept from looking as bedraggled as the rest of them was a mystery. It probably helped that he hadn't been in Texas long, which was one reason why he hadn't made many converts to his way of thinking. Most of the veteran hands resented the newcomers' aggressive certainty. But nobody liked running and the army had done nothing but run since Gonzales. If this went on much longer, he'd start making converts soon enough.

One thing that needed to be dealt right away with was something Sherman said the day before, although the Kentuckian didn't know that Houston was aware of it. Haranguing a group of men who were gathered under a cottonwood tree – the same tree they were under now - Sherman pointedly asked if a change in leadership might be the best way to win the war.

It was time to squelch the pipsqueak.

"To answer your question, Captain Sherman, strategy is not your responsibility. You are here to obey orders. Fight or retreat; it's not up to anyone but me. Any man caught disobeying orders or fomenting rebellion in the ranks will be tried for mutiny. And if found guilty, that man will be shot. Do I make myself clear?"

Houston pulled a twist of tobacco out of his coat pocket, cut off a chunk with a clasp knife, and popped it in his mouth. He'd only recently started chewing tobacco once or twice a day. He didn't particularly like it and probably never would, but it helped keep his mind off his need for a drink.

"Of course, I know that no man in this group would consider such a thing," he added, deliberately softening the threat to keep Sherman off balance.

When several officers smiled at the Kentuckian's discomfort, Houston knew he'd hit the target. None of them realized that he didn't have the stomach to shoot any of his own men, even a mutineer. He'd seen it done many years ago and he could never bring himself to do it, not now and not ever. But for all Sherman and the others knew, their general was the most bloodthirsty tyrant since Nero.

An expert reader of men from his time in politics, Houston assessed the senior officers gathered beneath the cottonwood's wide limbs and carefully weighed what he saw. Seguin, Smith and Karnes were with him and he knew it, all respected men who influenced others. And no man was more loyal than Hockley. Jesse Billingsley was a hard case who resembled an Old Testament prophet. He just wanted to fight; yesterday, today or tomorrow, it didn't matter, and he was growing impatient. The dour Ed Burleson believed himself to be command material and wouldn't mind a bit if Houston was pushed out. In a way, that helped Houston because Burleson would never follow Sherman. If Burleson wasn't offered command, then he would have no part in mutiny. Wylie Martin was an old friend of Buck Travis and was hot to avenge the death of his friend, constantly sneering about the army's "shameful retreat." Like Houston, Martin had served under Andrew Jackson at Horseshoe Bend, where he was a captain to Houston's mere lieutenant, and resented that Houston now had the superior rank. Martin was supported by his fellow officer and close friend, the very noisy Mosely Baker. Houston suspected that he might have to send those two off with some independent command before they poisoned the rest of the army. But not quite yet.

He hated having to worry as much about his own officers as he did about Santa Anna, but there was nothing to be done about it. Despite what many of them thought, he was not against battle in the right situation, but this probably wasn't it. If they fought and lost, the revolution was all but over. Win here and it wouldn't matter because they faced only one piece of Santa Anna's army. After taking heavy casualties, they'd only have to fight again. Santa Anna was the key. He was the one they had to beat.

But how? Where? When? Houston didn't tell anyone, not even Hockley or Smith, but he had no idea.

9

"BURNET DID WHAT?"

The only answer was silence. Even Smith looked like he didn't have the stomach to say any more.

"Don't blame us, General." The scout motioned to the three men who rode into camp with him. "When Burnet heard that Gaona was at Bastrop, he got all in a lather and took off like a scalded dog for Harrisburg over on Buffalo Bayou, He covered that seventy miles 'bout as fast as a man could, even with most of the cabinet coming along with him. Purty impressive performance."

Smith reached into the worn saddle bag he had slung over his shoulder, pulled out two letters, and handed them to Houston.

"Here's a letter from Burnet and another one from Tom Rusk, who wasn't real happy about bein' ordered to run. The problem is that some of our deserters got to Washington-on-the-Brazos, and all their scary stories about how bad things were sure didn't help Burnet's mood any. Accordin' to them, we don't ever intend to fight."

His mind churning, Houston left the camp and walked

upriver with Smith at his side and the other scouts trailing along behind. After about a hundred yards, he took a seat on a moss-covered rock, ripped open the letter and began to read. Burnet's blind panic was obvious in the words he'd written. In Harrisburg, the President and most of the cabinet – including de Zavala, Potter, Rusk, and Carson – were crammed into the home of Jane Harris, an elderly widow and mother of the town's founder. Against all logic and sound strategy, Burnet ordered Houston to abandon whatever plans he had and immediately proceed with the army to Harrisburg, the better to protect "government personnel."

"To protect David Burnet's pale white ass is what he means," grumbled Houston, who had no intention of following the ridiculous order. Still sitting on the rock, he leaned forward, put his elbows on his knees and cradled his chin in his hands, taking a moment to review a map of the countryside in his mind. Bastrop was at least sixty miles from Washington-on-the-Brazos. With all the swollen rivers and creeks in the way, it was at least a three day march for Gaona, so there was no reason for Burnet and the cabinet to run, especially all the way to Harrisburg. Hell, why not keep going all the way to New Orleans or Mobile? Besides, according to their best information, Gaona was headed to Nacogdoches, not Washington, though that could chance.

"Erastus, tell me, how are the people takin' it?" Houston straightened up, so infuriated he could barely get the question out. "They've got to know about this … this … flight of the *wise men* by now. A contagion like this can't help but catch on. What did you see on your way here?'

"They're runnin' like hell, too, most of 'em," Smith shrugged. "I figured you'd ask so me and the boys fanned out on the way back here to cover all the ground we could. We saw houses standin' open, meals left on tables, fires still burnin', and even stock left in corrals at a couple of places.

Some of the cribs were full of corn and the smokehouses full of bacon, all of it left behind to rot. Getting' here, we couldn't pass on some roads 'cause they was so jam full of people tryin' to get away with everything they could carry, even if they don't know what they were gettin' away from or goin' to. They figure if their government's runnin' the way it is and the army's retreatin', they should get the hell out. People got the runaway fever and they got it bad."

"Sweet Jesus." Houston rose to his feet. For the first time, he noticed Smith's exhaustion. "You'd best get yourself and your men some rest. It won't long before I'll be needin' you like I've never needed you before."

The scout nodded gratefully. "There's one more thing, General. He'll probably tell you that in the other letter, but in a few days Rusk aims to leave the cabinet to come join the army. He figures that he can do more good with us than with them. What he probably won't tell you is that while he don't like Burnet much, the President and some of the others want him to be the government's eyes and ears when he gets here."

"So what you're sayin' is that Tom Rusk is coming here to be Burnet's spy?"

Smith didn't bother to answer. He never liked saying the obvious.

———

THANKS to his absence of several days, Smith didn't know it, and Houston didn't tell him, but the situation was even worse than the scout knew. Just yesterday, Houston received a shocking report from Henry Karnes telling of Fannin's stunning defeat. Although he kept it quiet so not to discourage the men, he knew that it couldn't last much longer. Fannin's entire force, what was left of it, was imprisoned at Goliad. Houston had already written a letter to Rusk telling what he knew of the crushing loss. The courier had probably crossed paths with Smith on the way. With Rusk in Harrisburg, the letter would take a little longer to get to the Secretary of War, but it didn't change the cold facts.

Fannin had finally moved out of the *presidio* at Goliad, but, instead of discarding every bit of unnecessary equipment so that he could cover ground quickly, he took everything possible with him. The fool's baggage train was longer than his army. Against such a plodding retreat, the capable Urrea was too fast and too sure. Caught only six miles out of Goliad, as Urea's advance cavalry closed in Fannin ignored his officers' desperate pleas to get rid of everything that slowed them down and race ahead to Coleto Creek, which was literally within sight, where they could make a stand. Heavily wooded and with an unending source of water, it was an ideal defensive position.

Instead, Fannin decided to stop where he was, out on the open prairie with his 400 men facing Urrea's 1,400, or more. After ordering his men to form a hollow square, the fight started early in the afternoon and continued for the rest of the day, with Fannin's defenders desperately driving back charge after charge. Despite a painful wound in the thigh, the colonel refused to leave the front ranks and bravely fought alongside his men.

Houston remembered how he moaned as he read: If only the man's judgment was as sound as his courage was great.

By the end of the day, the Texians were suffering badly, with little food and no water. They'd taken sixty casualties while inflicting more than two hundred and fifty on the enemy. The canny Urrea had his sharpshooters concentrate on the men manning Fannin's cannon, so that within a few hours they were all dead or wounded. Urrea ordered the same *cazedores* to pick off Fannin's oxen and pack animals, too.

By nightfall, Urrea had Fannin right where he wanted him;

low on ball and powder, without a way to transport his wounded even if he could get away, and with little left in the way of food and no water at all.

After a terrible night that was punctuated by the moans and cries of the wounded, dawn revealed the grim picture; Fannin's suffering force was trapped in the middle of the open prairie with no where to run and no place to hide. Even worse, during the night Urrea brought up three cannon, which could blast the Texians to pieces at leisure.

Bowing to the inevitable, carrying a white flag Fannin limped forward out of his pitiful position. There was conflicting information about the terms, although Houston suspected the worst. When Fannin returned to his men, he said that their lives would be spared. They probably would be paroled and sent home as long as they pledged never again to raise arms against Mexico. But Houston knew that Santa Anna's standing orders were to kill all captured rebels. Urrea might disagree with those orders. From everything Houston heard about the man he probably did. But there was nothing he could do. Houston suspected that Fannin lied to his men about the terms, hoping to somehow negotiate later to try and save as many of their lives as possible.

James Fannin's once formidable force of 400 fighting men had ceased to exist.

"You know that I am not easily depressed," Houston wrote to Rusk. "But before God I have found these to be among the darkest hours of my life. If what I have heard about Fannin be true, I can only attribute the ill luck to his attempt to retreat in daylight in the face of a superior force. He is an ill-fated man."

Houston passed the letter to Hockley to have a courier deliver it to the Secretary of War. With a grim nod toward his own small, untrained army, he whispered, "Hockley, what you see there is the last hope of Texas."

10

"WHERE DO you think they're takin' us now, Zachariah?"

"I don't know any more than you do, boy," replied Zachariah Barns, who, at a grizzled 47, was more than twice the age of his young friend, Nathaniel Kemper. "But I heard a rumor they might be marchin' us to the coast. Once we're there we'll give our parole then get put on a ship and sent back home, probably to New Orleans first off."

Kemper took a deep luxurious breath. After the fight near Coleto Creek where Colonel Fannin had to surrender and more than likely saved all their lives, the men were marched back to Goliad where they were confined indoors for eight long days, with too many men jammed into too few rooms. It felt good to be outside after so long of being penned up like chickens in a coop. If old Barns was right, it looked like the humiliation of captivity was almost over. After a short march to the coast, they'd all be able to breathe ocean air instead of their own stink. Coming from Charleston as he did, Kemper missed the ocean.

Sensing sudden movement among the men, Kemper stood

on his toes to try to see over the tightly packed crowd of prisoners outside the *presidio* walls.

"What's happenin' now?" he asked.

Five inches taller than Kemper, Barns peered over the heads of the men in front.

"Looks like they're dividin' us into groups," he said.

"How come?"

"Don't know. Maybe they think it'll make us easier to manage on the march."

As they always did, Barns and Kemper managed to stay together while Fannin's men were divided into four groups. Kemper was grateful for Barns' companionship. He did not think he would have survived the fight at Coleto Creek and the horror of that night without Barns' steady experience to guide him.

Closely guarded on both sides, their group of 80 ragged men left the *presidio* and marched a half mile to the San Antonio River, which seemed strange because the road to the coast went the other way. Prodded by the *soldados'* bayonets, they were herded shoulder to shoulder to the river shore, where the Mexican officers barked out orders and the *soldados* quickly formed a ragged line facing the prisoners.

For the first time, Kemper noticed the unusual quiet. Usually the Mexicans were a talkative bunch, but not today. Except for the officers' orders, the silence was almost eerie.

Now that they were out in the open, he saw that there was no baggage or baggage train with them, as if they weren't marching very far at all. And it was strange how the Mexicans were all in their parade best.

Kemper started to mention all this to Barnes when an odd look came over the older man's weathered face. He shoved Kemper to the ground, and jumped forward so he was between his friend and the Mexican line.

Before Kemper could protest, or ask what was happening,

Barnes yelled in a tone that Kemper had never heard from him before, "Stay down boy! After they fire, break for the river as fast as you can!"

The bewildered Kemper heard some shouting and then an officer bellowed, "Fuego!" followed by a fearful crash the like of which he'd never experienced, not even at Coleto Creek. It seemed to stun the sense out of him.

Barnes reeled and fell back against the younger man, which caused them both to sag to the ground. As they fell, Kemper caught Barnes around the chest and it was only when his hands came back bloody that he realized what was happening.

"They're goin' to murder us all!"

With the wails of the wounded, the cries of the Mexicans, and the sound of heavy firing from somewhere not too distant, Kemper could barely hear his own voice.

He stayed still underneath Barns' body while the *soldados*, bayonets at the ready, charged over the dead and wounded to kill those survivors who were trying to escape. Once the murderous wave passed, Kemper wiggled free and raced diagonally toward the river, away from the mass of bodies.

As he ran, it was as if time slowed down and he could see everything around him in great clarity and detail.

He saw a captain named Holland hit a Mexican with his fist. Holland wrenched the stunned soldier's rifle from his hands, clubbed him with it, and ran for his life.

He saw the Mexican cavalry ride down at least a dozen fleeing men and butcher them with their lances. They made it look like sport.

Off to his left, he saw three men desperately racing to the river. One was killed on the shore when the point of a lance entered his back and burst out of his chest. A second was shot down in knee-deep water, falling forward on his face. The third man abruptly changed course and began running parallel to the river. Kemper never saw him again.

Just as Kemper reached the water, a hard blow on the side of his head knocked him to his knees. Knowing that he had to keep moving or die, he rolled over, jumped to his feet, and grappled with a Mexican officer who was waving a sword. He kneed the officer in the groin and pulled away. He made a frantic dash to the river and dived into the shallows, scraping his chest on the rocky bottom while musket balls splashed all around him.

Raised on ocean, Kemper was a good swimmer and stayed underwater until he thought his lungs would burst. When he finally surfaced, he found himself out in the middle of the river. Feigning death, he floated on his stomach and let the current carry him downstream until he was finally out of range.

He didn't know it, but he was one of only thirty men who escaped that day. Only six made it to Houston's army to tell what happened on that terrible Palm Sunday.

James Fannin was not among them. Unable to walk or even stand as a result of his festering leg wound, he was one of forty wounded men who were executed separately in Goliad. Once he learned of his fate, Fannin requested that he be shot in the chest and not in the head, that his valuable watch be sent to his family, and that he be given a Christian burial. He calmly tied on his own blindfold and faced the firing squad sitting on a chair.

Colonel James Fannin was shot in the face and his body thrown on a funeral pyre with the other victims. The officer in charge of the execution pocketed the watch.

"YOU KNOW, Hockley, as terrible as this news is, it might work in our favor," mused Houston, raising a tin cup to his lips and taking a sip of coffee that he discovered had about the same flavor as boiled weeds.

As Hockley tentatively took a sip of his own, a shocked look passed across his face. He set his cup on the ground beside the worn saddle he was sitting on. Houston, who was sitting on the ground with his back against a tree, couldn't tell if his aide was shocked by what he said, or by the coffee.

"You see, Urrea was smarter than Santa Anna," Houston explained, tossing the awful brew aside with a flick of his wrist. "If he'd been allowed to parole Fannin's men like I hear he wanted, we'd have near four hundred demoralized men running loose, babbling about how Santa Anna is invincible and maybe we should lay down our arms and surrender so he won't kill us all. With most of the population already in a panic, it wouldn't take long for such an idea to get some serious traction."

Houston saw that the bright young aide had caught his meaning.

"Now even the faintest of hearts among us know better," Houston continued. "We either win, or we die. There is no peace party anymore, not one that matters. With what he did to Fannin and his men, Santa Anna showed all of us that there is no middle ground."

There was a comfortable silence between them while Hockley digested it all. The camp's fires were long since out and the night was punctuated by the snores of hundreds of sleeping men. As usual, Houston couldn't sleep. He doubted that he'd slept more than three hours at a stretch since the campaign began.

"What will we do now, sir?"

Houston slowly got to his feet and looked around the sleeping camp.

"Despite what I just said, for now we neither fight nor die." He pulled an old watch out of his waistcoat pocket and checked the time. "Later on today we're going into the retreatin' business again."

"Most of the men won't be happy about that," Hockley said.

"No" Houston admitted. "No, they will not."

11

AND SO THE army of Texas fell back yet again. This time it was headed to San Felipe. From there, Houston intended to move north along the Brazos River to Groce's Plantation.

Houston pushed the cursing and complaining men hard through the driving rain. With the terrible weather, it was impossible to keep them organized in a decent line. Rain came down in driving cascades that seemed to beat a man into the ground. Mules and horses bogged down in the mud and men slid off the trail into the brush from sheer exhaustion, despite staff officers constantly riding up and down the long column shouting, "Close up! Close up!"

After sloshing along for 30 miles, when the exhausted army bivouacked at San Felipe a rumor swept through the ranks that Houston was so intent on avoiding a battle with the enemy that he intended to retreat all the way to the Sabine River, and perhaps even cross the river into the United States.

It *was* true that Houston had been in contact with General Edmund Gaines, the US Army commander at Fort Jessup in Natchitoches. For that matter, so had Texas Secretary of State Sam Carson, who'd traveled to Natchitoches to meet with

Gaines. While the United States could not officially engage Mexico, Carson wanted to prove that Santa Anna's government was working with the Indians along the border, encouraging and supporting the tribes committing atrocities on both sides of the Sabine River. In a letter to Houston, Carson explained that he'd try to make Gaines understand how he "could maintain the honor of his country and still cross the Sabine and move on the aggressors," which Carson hoped to successfully identify as Santa Anna and his "minions."

Although Gaines agreed to move 600 men to the Sabine, he was determined not to enter Texas until circumstances justified it or he received orders from Washington. While it might be possible to provoke a border incident with Mexico and draw United States troops across the river, Houston doubted that it would happen in time do much good. Win or lose, the revolution would likely be over by then.

In the meantime, Carson urged Houston not to fight if he could avoid it. *"You must fall back, and hold out, and let nothing goad or provoke you to a battle, unless you can, without doubt, whip them, or unless you are compelled to fight."*

The mass of conflicting information, unrealistic expectations, and amateur strategy neatly summarized Houston's maddening dilemma. At the same time he was ridiculed by many of his officers and government officials, including President Burnet, for avoiding a fight, there were others, including Secretary of State Carson, who wanted him to hold off and either wait for the United Sates to get involved or until the long-expected new recruits arrived from across the border. Although the army wasn't ready to fight a full engagement against Santa Anna's battle-hardened veterans, Houston doubted that he could wait long enough for either one of the other two options to bear fruit.

It didn't help the morale of his men that, according to another bizarre rumor, their general had become an opium addict, which explained his puzzling behavior and policy of retreat. It was so silly that Houston didn't bother to deny it. He'd learned a long time ago that people rarely let facts get in the way of a good rumor. The shaky foundation of this rumor was the result of his keeping a vial of ammoniacal spirits made by distilling liquid from the shavings of deer horns, an old Cherokee nostrum for warding off colds and other illness. With all the terrible weather, Houston sniffed the vial so regularly that it caused some of the army's denser clods to believe that he took opium.

While they rested at San Felipe during a respite from the rain, Houston was assaulted with so many civilian and military requests, demands, details, and entreaties at times he felt that just one more might send him screaming into the woods. He tried to escape late at night by reading one of the only two books he had with him, worn copies of *Gulliver's Travels* and an edition of *Caesar's Commentaries*. So far, he hadn't been able to find a copy of *The Iliad*, a lifelong favorite.

One bearskin wearing lunatic wandered into camp claiming to be the son of God. As such, he claimed to have important information and demanded to see Houston straightaway. When Hockley relayed the mad man's "request," the usually sober aide laughed so hard that he couldn't speak and it took him three tries to get it all out. Once Houston understood, he joined in; general and aide giggling like school girls.

"Please tell the man that I would be delighted to see him, but first would he mind providing a letter of recommendation from his father," said Houston, still snorting with laughter.

Much more serious was a report that a blind widow named Mary Millsaps, whose husband was killed at the Alamo, and her six – or was it seven? - children were trapped on their small hardscrabble farm more than 30 miles south.

Apparently they had been bypassed or somehow overlooked in the army's long retreat.

Houston summoned Juan Seguin to his makeshift tent, a section of canvass stretched between the limbs of two trees that provided some shelter while he dealt with the details of running the army.

When the bedraggled *Tejano* rode into camp and presented himself, boots caked in mud and sombrero soggy from the rain, Houston apologized before giving the order.

"Juan, I don't know for sure if this woman even exists, but we sure as the devil can't leave a blind widow of the Alamo and her brats to the mercy of the elements, the Mexicans, or even our fellow Texians, some of whom are usual the chaos to break all the laws there are." Houston saw Seguin steel himself for what he knew was coming. "Can you send a detail of, say, three of your men to find this woman, if she exists, and get her the hell out of harm's way?"

"And where might that be, General?" asked Seguin sarcastically.

"Damned if I know," Houston admitted. "With luck, maybe you'll know when you see it."

———

Too soon, it was time to leave San Felipe behind, only the army would do it without Mosely Baker, Wiley Martin, and over 200 of their men. Houston hated to lose the men, but knew that if he ordered the two stubborn firebrands to retreat any further they would only defy it. If he allowed mutiny take hold at such a high level more than likely he would lose control of the army.

But it was hard to give up San Felipe. As Stephen Austin's original town, it was the hub of American settlement in Texas. Wiley Martin was one of Austin's original settlers, known as the "old three hundred," and years ago had served as San Felipe's *alcalde*. Thinking with their hearts and not their heads, as usual, some of the men thought that the little town should be held at all costs.

After another mostly sleepless night, Houston found a solution that was so remarkably devious that it gave him pleasure. It reminded him of the old days of politicking back in Tennessee. If Martin and Baker wouldn't consent to fall back with the rest of the army, at least he'd found a way to get some use out of them, hastily scribbling orders that Baker's 120 men would take up a defensive position along the river ford at San Felipe while Martin's 100 men would move 30 miles downstream to the crossing at Fort Bend. With that, the two best river crossings in the area would be ably defended by men who were eager to fight and help delay the Mexican pursuit. At the same time, it got Baker and Martin away from the rest of the men, where they couldn't spread their mutinous poison. If they wanted to fight so badly, let them fight where it would do the most good.

Just as important, at least to the rank and file, the whole thing looked like their general's idea. Instead of looking weak, he seemed stronger than ever.

But before leaving San Felipe, Houston had to reassure the men that the running would stop, that he had a plan in mind and it was in their best interest to put their faith in it. At the same time, it had to be done indirectly so he wouldn't seem to be explaining himself or asking for approval. Knowing that it would spread like prairie fire, he pretended to let slip his long-range plan, specifically that they were headed to the large plantation of Jared Groce. One of the richest planters in Texas, Groce had always been generous in his support of the revolution. Once there, the army would rest and drill before finally launching its offensive.

At least that's what Houston let out. It wasn't a lie, exactly.

It just wasn't the whole truth. He did intend to bide his time at Groce's while the army gathered strength, but beyond that he had no idea what he might do. Something would turn up, of that he was confident. In his experience, if he was patient enough something always did, assuming he had the brains to recognize it and the ability to take advantage of it.

Privately, he feared for San Felipe once the army marched away. Austin founded the settlement on the west bank of the Brazos, without any thought of using the river as a defense against an enemy moving in from the west. Baker's orders were to defend the ford, not the town, and he would do that from the east bank, waiting to pounce on the enemy as it attempted to cross the river.

Preferring to leave nothing behind for the Mexicans, Houston considered telling Karnes to burn the town once the army was safely away, but decided against it. The melancholy sight of Gonzales blazing in the night was too fresh in his memory.

But after a day's march north, Houston learned that San Felipe had burned to the ground and its citizens were on the run, just like what sometimes seemed like every man, woman, and child in Texas. He didn't know if San Felipe was put to the torch on Baker's order or by the townspeople themselves because they knew how vulnerable they were on the wrong side of the river and refused to leave their homes for the enemy.

Either way, he confessed to Hockley that it didn't matter.

"If we didn't burn it," he said, "the Mexicans would."

12

WELL, halleluiah! It looked like they were getting two cannon, courtesy of the good folks in far off Cincinnati.

According to a letter from Ed Harcourt, the reliable Dutchman Houston appointed the army's chief engineer - a grand title hiding the fact that Harcourt had no resources whatsoever - the cannon had already arrived in Galveston by way of New Orleans. In a brief dispatch, Harcourt said that he'd have them delivered to Groce's as soon as he could find decent teams of horses to haul them.

That might take a while, Houston thought as he set the dispatch aside. With the population running, the army marching, and Santa Anna pursuing, decent mounts were hard to find these days. Still, the cannon were something he could use to encourage the men, a sign that they hadn't been forgotten by the rest of the world. They could use a little encouragement, too, sick as they were of all the drilling and training they'd endured lately. He had them out every day and intended to work them until he was sure that they would obey battlefield orders without having to think about it.

To make sure that no trooper or officer could claim that

they didn't know the orders, or somehow misunderstood them, Houston had the long list of daily routine posted in several places throughout camp. Most of it was basic military procedure, although many of the men groused they were much abused by the few common-sense rules:

1. *Roll call at reveille (5 o'clock) and tattoo (9 o'clock), when all light will be put out except in the tents of the officers employed on duty.*
2. *Silence will be preserved after tattoo.*
3. *At the first taps of the drum, each man will take his place in line.*
4. *In case of an alarm, the men will form on their ground and await orders.*
5. *The officer of the day will make the guard rounds at 9, 12 and 4 o'clock in the night. He will receive the watch word from the commanding officer and communicate the same.*
6. *Guards to be mounted and relieved at 9 a.m.*
7. *No sentinel will sit down on post, unless ordered.*
8. *The guard will be responsible for all prisoners put in custody.*
9. *Any person quitting camp, without leave, will be regarded as a deserted and treated as such.*
10. *To desert or sleep on post will be death by law.*
11. *No man is to pass the lines with arms, unless passed by a field officer.*
12. *The field officers of the regiment, the general, and his staff only have power to pass persons through the lines.*
13. *13. The men always to parade with arms, and to sleep with their arms in their reach.*
14. *No shooting within one mile of camp, or on march without leave.*

15. *All horses are to be brought within the line of sentinels before dark.*
16. *All expresses arriving in camp, and all intelligence, will first report to the commander in chief.*
17. *All horses arriving in camp will be staked down, tied, or close hobbled. Those that may not be attended to will be liable to be condemned to the public use.*
18. *Persons arriving in camp will immediately report to the colonel and be attached to some company for duty.*
19. *The sick of each company, platoon, or squad will report themselves to their respective officers, who will report them to the surgeon.*

It is ordered that the above regulations be strictly observed and obeyed.
    Sam Houston
    Com'r in chief

When Houston discovered than no one knew how to beat reveille or tattoo on the army's old drum, he decided to do it himself. It did the men good to see that their general was up before they were and still awake when they turned in.

The men didn't know it, but Houston took pains not to over-drill the men. He wanted the army well trained, not exhausted. The march through the fetid Brazos River bottom was punishing and Groce's was the first real rest most of them had in weeks. Fortunately, while they still had too many deserters - men unable to keep up, men desperate to find their families, or men who wanted no more part in what seemed like a losing war - even more came to take their place until Houston had about 900 men. The generous Jared Groce somehow found a way to feed them all from his gardens and herds. When Houston admitted that he had no money to pay for it all, the planter just shrugged and replied that the government's poverty wasn't exactly a secret and that the army should pay what it could when it could. Groce's blacksmith shop became their armory and he had a supply of scarce lead pipes melted down to make rifle balls. The spectacular plantation house was turned over to the army surgeon, a newcomer named Nicholas Descomps Labadie, for a hospital.

Valuable as he was, Houston didn't like Labadie. He considered the man to be a pompous *poseur* and knew that the French Canadian returned the favor, saying much the same thing about the general to anyone who'd listen. In his more generous moments, Houston conceded that maybe they were both right.

But there was no denying that Labadie was good at what he did and the army was lucky to have him. After weeks of constant exposure and hard marching, many of the men were so sick they could barely stand, and others couldn't stand at all. Influenza, whooping cough, pink eye, measles, mumps, diarrhea, dysentery, and a variety of other known and unknown infirmities all seemed to conspire to do Santa Anna's work for him. They'd been on the move so much that the government didn't know where to send what supplies, medicine, and reinforcements it could gather. Now that they'd stopped a while, they were receiving small quantities of everything, even including a few tents. Just yesterday, a surprise shipment of almost 200 badly needed pairs of shoes came in.

At the moment, Houston's biggest worry was his own government. The long-expected Tom Rusk had finally ridden into camp. What wasn't expected was the scathing letter he delivered from David Burnet. Written in the President's typical blustering style, Houston knew that he must have the support of most of the cabinet or he wouldn't have sent it:

Sir, the enemy are laughing you to scorn. You must fight them.

You must retreat no further. The country expects you to fight. The salvation of the country depends on your doing so."

Houston controlled his anger – with Rusk newly arrived in camp he felt that he had to - but it wasn't easy to read such high and mighty words from a man who galloped pell-mell out of Washington-on-the-Brazos at the first sign that there might be a Mexican trooper within 50 miles. He knew that he wasn't popular in some quarters, sometimes with good reason. There was no denying it. He drank too much and got too drunk too often back at the constitutional convention. But if anyone deserved to be laughed "to scorn," it was David Burnet.

But right now Houston faced a crisis of another sort. According to his informants in the cabinet, Tom Rusk was authorized to relieve him of command and take control of the army if he deemed it necessary. Their meeting later today may be the most important of his life. Everything – everything! - hinged on the outcome. If he didn't command, who would? Rusk had no experience. Call it vanity, as many did, but Houston was sure that he could somehow lead this army to victory. But if he was relieved and tossed aside like so much trash, Houston knew that he would more than likely sink into alcohol before fading into obscurity. He'd already been there and didn't like it. And this time he would never escape. A man only had so many chances in life. He had to win Rusk over this afternoon, he simply had to.

————

BEFORE THEY SAT down to talk it through, Houston took Rusk on a tour of the camp so that the newcomer could see how both morale and heath were improving. True, the men grumbled about everything under the sun and they had plenty to grumble about. But the men in all armies grumbled. It was a soldier's way.

At the same time, the few casual minutes spent with Rusk gave Houston a chance to assess the man who had the power to change his life. In his early 30s, the South Carolinian seemed to possess an eager intelligence. Of middling height, he had dark hair and only a nose just this side of bulbous kept him from being considered handsome. Like Houston, he was a lawyer, a protégé of Jackson's deadly enemy, John Calhoun. Rusk came to Texas with no intention of settling. The managers of a Georgia mining company in which he'd invested embezzled the money and fled across the border, with Rusk in angry pursuit. He found the men, but not the money, in Nacogdoches and decided to stay. In Houston's recollection, he always got along with Rusk well enough and was confident that Rusk would at least listen to what he had to say. He might not agree with all of it, but at least he'd listen.

It was supper time as they wound their way through camp, with cooking fires burning as the men prepared their usual meal of beef – salt was scarce, as usual - and corn. In addition to the beef ration, every man was issued one ear of corn each day. Some of the men cooked it on the fire with the beef and ate it by the ear. Others preferred to grind it in one of the small mills issued to each company, then dump it in an iron skillet and cook it into mush. Houston usually carried an ear or two in his coat pocket and gnawed on one when he got hungry.

"You know, Tom, I was looking through *Caesar's Commentaries* last night, and read that Julius Caesar wore a red cloak into battle. I was struck by that fact because ... Boy, what in the hell are you doin' with that old rifle?"

Houston stopped before a young man, not much older than his mid-teens, who was on his knees struggling to repair a wet rifle that wouldn't fire. To Houston's expert eye, the problem was as obvious as the solution. The youngster just didn't have the first notion what was wrong or how to go about fixing it.

Expecting to receive a hiding from his famously hot-tempered general, the private seemed to shrink in on himself. Instead, Houston gently took the weapon out of the soldier's trembling hands and walked to a nearby fire.

"Let me take a look, if you don't mind," Houston said, hefting the rifle in his big hands. "During my years runnin' a tradin' post up on Neosho River, I was a fair gunsmith, if I do say so myself. Mostly I had to be. There wasn't anybody around to do it for me. Let me show you how it's done, at least if I remember correctly."

Houston sat down beside the fire, crossed his long legs and cradled the rifle in his lap.

"You don't happen to have a pocket handkerchief, do you?" Seeing the soldier's puzzled look, Houston muttered, "No, I 'spose not."

An amused Rusk reached over Houston's shoulder and offered his own handkerchief. Taking it, the general continued, "First off, you warm the handkerchief by the fire. Once that's done, you take the rifle and open the pan, like this." Houston's expert hands moved over the weapon as if they had their own memory. "You wrap the warm handkerchief around the lock and let it remain for a few seconds. Repeat that two or three times and this old rifle of yours should be good as new."

Finishing, Houston handed the weapon and handkerchief to the soldier. The young man reached out to return the handkerchief to Rusk, but the secretary of war refused it.

"I think you'd better hang on to it, private. Keeping that rifle in good condition is the best use I can think of for that old piece of cloth," Rusk said with a grin. "Who knows, it might save my life one day."

Amid laughter and applause from the men, Rusk and Houston left the fire and ambled through the camp to Houston's new tent, which was considerably bigger than the tattered old one he left back in Gonzales. Rusk accepted a cigar and Houston lit one for himself, part of a shipment of supplies that came in from Brazoria two days ago. In short order, the tent was filled with smoke like a foggy day.

"I'd offer you a libation, but I've sworn off for the duration of the campaign," Houston said.

"I heard that," Rusk nodded. "I hope you won't be offended if I say that I'm impressed at your sacrifice."

"I'm impressed myself," Houston admitted. "And I hope that I can continue to be impressive."

And so, in the most oblique way possible, they got down to the real subject of their meeting. The time passed quickly. While Rusk asked a few questions, Houston did most of the talking, including his ideas about trading land for time as he drew Santa Anna further east and stretched the lines that separated the various parts of the Mexican army, waiting for the Mexican president to make a mistake. The fate of the Alamo and Goliad only confirmed his suspicions about the pathetically disorganized government's inability to support garrisons separated by great distances.

"It would be madness to try to hold a fixed position with these troops," he declared, thumping his fist on his thigh for emphasis. "Our forces must not be shut up where the can neither be supplied with men nor provisions."

An hour after they began, Houston concluded, "And if I haven't convinced you, Tom, well, then I just haven't. There's nothing more to say, and that's a rare thing for me. In the few years we've known each other, you've always struck me as a reasonable, fair-minded man, and I'm counting on that now. I'm sure you've heard enough anti-Houston rhetoric to last a lifetime."

"Several lifetimes, I'd say," Rusk admitted. "When he talks about you, Burnet uses words like 'military fop' and 'miserable imbecility.'"

"He must have been leafing through Mister Webster's dictionary again," Houston said with a grin. "I suppose that's a fair exchange for the things I've called him."

"I'd say you're still well ahead," Rusk observed. "Burnet's not the dolt you think he is, general. He just doesn't have your nimble way with words. Not many do."

Rusk leaned back and laced his fingers behind his head. It had grown dark and the tent was lit by a single lantern.

"I suspect that you know the main reason why I'm here. Such secrets are hard to keep. Make no mistake, general, I do intend to join the army, but my instructions stipulate that if I don't take the, ah, *other* action by taking command, stopping the retreat, and bringing us into battle, I am to remain with you as an observer reporting to the administration."

"By the way," he asked, "who is your spy in the cabinet? You must have at least one, maybe more. My guess is de Zavala, but that's only a guess."

Houston took a deep draw on his second cigar of the night before he answered. "I regret all this spying on each other, but I'm afraid that the times make it necessary. You do Lorenzo a disservice. He's too honorable to do anything so base. Besides, if I told you who he is, he wouldn't be much of a spy, would he? Or maybe it is Lorenzo? After all, wouldn't I deny it if it was?"

Laughing, Rusk threw up his hands. "All right, Sam. I give up. And I don't think you regret the spying, not one bit. If anything, I think you enjoy the intrigue. Once again, I see that your reputation is richly deserved."

"Which reputation is that?"

"All of them, I think."

73

Houston dropped the light-hearted banter. "Tom, I have a proposition for you, if you're open to one."

Rusk waved his hand as a sign to continue.

"I propose that you join this army as planned, only as a full colonel. That way, instead of spying for David Burnet you'll be working for me. I can only promise you poor food, miserable conditions, and a decent chance that you'll be killed or wounded. What do you say?"

Rusk stared deep into Houston's eyes, weighing the possibilities. Houston stared back, refusing to be the first to lower his gaze.

Rusk got to his feet and offered his hand.

"General, how could anyone refuse such a persuasive offer?" he said. "I accept."

13

WHILE HOUSTON and Rusk came to their surprising agreement, Mosely Baker, Wiley Martin, and their men struggled with problems of their own: Independent command was not as easy at it looked and Santa Anna was a stouter foe than any of them imagined.

To defend the ford at San Felipe, as ordered Baker's company dug in on the east side of the Brazos, across from the settlement's fire-blackened ruins. After both sides glared at each for a while from opposite sides of the river, the Mexicans brought up two field pieces and began shelling Baker's breastworks. At the same time, Santa Anna's riflemen laid down an accurate fire that killed one of Baker's men.

To keep the enemy from getting across the Brazos, Baker's men searched both sides of the river to commandeer, hide, or destroy anything that floated. Despite those efforts, the Mexicans managed to locate an old abandoned flatboat. Encouraged by their find, they patched it up and began building two more, using what unburned logs and planks they found in the ruins of San Felipe. But when it came time to launch the three craft, Baker's sharpshooters fired across the river with such deadly accuracy that it all came to nothing.

Stalemate.

————

"THE CAPTAIN WANTS us to do *what?*" asked Will Simpson, who was certain that he hadn't heard right.

Isaac Hill and James Bell looked at each other, and then looked at Simpson, who was always the weakest link in their very short chain.

"You suddenly growed hard of hearing like old Deaf Smith?" asked Hill. "The three of us are assigned picket duty. We are to cross the river and keep our eyes open and our ears flappin' in case the Mexicans do anything suspicions."

Simpson still couldn't believe it. Why did they have to cross the river for that? When were Mexicans ever anything but suspicious? A man sure didn't have to be up close to see it. An assignment of such dangerous nature wasn't what he had in mind, not at all. The only reason he volunteered to join Mosely Baker's men, leave the main army, and march here was to get away from that damned old windbag Houston and all the marching here and there and drilling and marching some more while officers shouted at a man and demanded that he do things he didn't want to do and didn't understand why he should.

Will Simpson didn't join the army to be shouted at. He didn't join to fight either, which he never mentioned to anyone, especially Hill and Bell, who actually seemed to want to take on Santa Anna and his thousands of bloodthirsty Mexicans. He joined only after he heard about Houston's habit of retreat, which, in Simpson's view, made him nothing short of a military genius. In these uncertain times, what could be safer than to be surrounded by armed men in an army that never fought a battle? True, most of the men wanted to fight. So let the crack brains fight while he watched from afar. Putting himself in harm's way, which sounded like what was about to happen with this cross-the-river-and-watch-the-Mexicans nonsense, was never Simpson's intention.

Why, oh, why didn't he have the sense to stay home in North Carolina? To tell the truth, he knew the answer perfectly well. It started when Theodosia's father came roaring at him late one night with a loaded shotgun demanding that he marry his daughter, considering the family way in which he put her, as if it was all his fault. The old man interrupted a sound sleep, too.

As he assessed the situation later that night, once he talked the old bastard out of his murderous rage, Texas began to look pretty good, at least until now. The next morning, like many of his neighbors, he scrawled GTT – Gone to Texas – on the door of his little cabin fives miles outside of Charlotte and got the hell out. Let Theodosia and her dangerous father fend for themselves, by God!

And now here he was. All things considered, it didn't seem like much improvement at all.

The three men crossed the river under the cover of darkness and tied their canoe to a tree, where it was hidden by low-hanging limbs but easily found if they had to leave in a hurry. Ignoring Simpson's hopeful observation that they need go no further because once the sun came up they could more than likely see plenty of suspicious behavior from right here, they positioned themselves just east of what used to be the town and about three-quarters of a mile in from the river. As Hill explained it, they were to watch all through the long day until they were relieved that night by three other lunatics.

They drew straws for the watch, which would be positioned about thirty yards closer to the Mexican camp than the other two sleeping men. Bell and Hill drew the first two watches and Simpson the third. It was hard for Simpson to get to sleep knowing that a whole army that wanted to kill him was almost close enough to hear the men fart, but sleep he did in fits and starts He didn't even snore as much as he usually did, mostly because either Hill or Bell kicked him in the ribs every time he started, which seriously cut into his relaxation.

Having the third watch, Simpson was supposed to wake the others at dawn so they could change position to a more secluded spot, but events took an unfortunate turn; the unfortunate turn being that Simpson fell asleep when he should have been watching. Bell and Hill were awaked by the sound of horses that were much too close and getting closer. Seizing their weapons and rising to their knees to cautiously peer over the tall river grass, they saw Mexican cavalry less than 100 yards away.

The noise startled Simpson awake, too. Well, almost awake. Instead of rising cautiously like the others, the confused guard jumped to his feet and shouted, "Oh, of course, I love you most," which Hill and Bell later surmised was a remnant of a dream, and probably quite a pleasurable one, or at least working up to it.

Riding in from opposites sides, two Mexican cavalrymen lassoed Simpson just as he was getting his feet under him to run. While admiring the accuracy of Mexican rope work, seeing their companion trussed up like a pig ready for market and with nothing they could do about it, Hill and Bell raced for the Brazos and the safety of their canoe. Paddling furiously, they made it across, but just barely, with rifle balls plopping into the water all around them while the *soldados* on the river bank shouted taunts, which didn't matter because neither man could speak Spanish and wouldn't have cared even if they understood.

One of Deaf Smith's Spanish-speaking scouts, who knew several of the scores of civilians that were hanging around Santa Anna's army to do laundry, mending, and other labor, reported that Simpson told the Mexicans everything he knew about the Texian force, which wasn't much except for the fact that most of the army had retreated to Groce's Plantation. It was Santa Anna's first accurate information about Houston's whereabouts in weeks. Knowing that he had to find a way across the river, leaving Sesma with enough men to hold Baker in place, Santa Anna led a column toward Thompson's Ferry, not far above Fort Bend, where Martin's defenders were dug in.

When the Mexican vanguard spotted a ferryman on the opposite shore, Santa Anna and his staff hid in the woods while the suave Colonel Juan Almonte, who spoke English, Spanish, and French with equal ease, stepped confidently up to the shore and hailed the ferryman. Thinking that casually dressed Almonte was a Texian who was trying to catch up to the army, the ferryman poled the ferry back across the river to the west bank. When the ferry crashed ashore, Santa Anna and his staff sprang out of the brush to capture the ferryman and, more important, his ferry, which allowed the Mexicans to make a bloodless crossing of the river, although it took several days to do it.

Twelve miles away, when Martin and his men at the Fort Bend crossing learned that the Mexicans were across the river in force and that they'd been outflanked, they had no choice but to fall back. Up at San Felipe, when Baker was confronted with the same information, he did the same thing.

With both commands now in full flight toward Groce's and Santa Anna across the river, all the defenders had to show for their bravado was one casualty and two prisoners taken by the Mexicans; the ferryman and Will Simpson.

No one knew if Simpson was tortured before he talked,

but those who knew him doubted it very much. They never saw him again.

————

"HE'S IGNORIN' us, General."

"Really?" asked a surprised Houston. "Why?"

"The way I heard it, Santa Anna figures he can always scoop us up," replied Smith, who was just returned from anther long scout. "Considerin' that he's already whipped us at the Alamo and Goliad, with Urrea snatchin' up the coast settlements right and left, and that we've done nuthin' but run, he don't have much respect for us. "

Houston shot a hard look at Smith and the scout raised his hands as if to ward off the general's pique.

"I'm just reportin'. Ain't none of it personal."

"I do know it, Erastus, and I apologize," Houston said. "You didn't deserve that. You just keep on tellin' me what you know."

As usual when Smith made one of his reports, for privacy they met in Houston's tent, where the scout gratefully accepted a handful of cigars and stuffed them in his pocket.

"If not us, then what is he after?" Houston asked.

"The cabinet; the whole damn government if he can get it," answered Smith. "He figures that if he can capture them boys, it's all over 'cause we'll have no more government to fight for. We'll be so dem … demorized … what's the word?"

"Demoralized?" suggested Houston.

"That's it," nodded Smith. "We'll be so demoralized this army will just about blow away on the wind. Those that don't run can always be taken easy enough."

"Damn!" muttered Houston. "He just may be right, too."

Houston told himself that being underestimated by the

enemy might work in his favor, but he still didn't like it. To be dismissed like this was damned insulting.

"General, the good news is that there's not much of the cabinet left in one place for Santa Anna to grab. There's only three of 'em at Harrisburg. Burnet and de Zavala both left to attend to their families. Potter's over at Galveston Bay, doing whatever a secretary of navy does. And you know Carson's in Louisiana.

"The other thing is that Nacogdoches and San Augustine are both 'bout empty of people, so there's no reason for Santa Anna, or any of his other generals, to bother with either one. There's thousands of older men, women, and children hidin' in the woods along both sides of the Sabine. The truth is they don't know where else to go and probably couldn't get there even if they did."

Houston rubbed his fingers across his forehead while he thought it through. As unexpected as Santa Anna's new strategy was Houston's first move was obvious.

"Erastus, I'd appreciate it if you'd have one of your boys find Henry Karnes and bring him here. I need him to find Burnet and tell him what Santa Anna's up to. It may be time for the President to run some more."

14

WEARY OF HIS long pursuit of the rebel army and longing to be back at his comfortable home in Vera Cruz, Antonio Lopez de Santa Anna and his advance guard stopped at an inn on the San Bernardo River owned by Elizabeth Powell.

One of the few settlers who had not fled during what was already known as the Runaway Scrape, the widow was forced to feed Santa Anna and his staff. As usual, the common soldiers were left to fend for themselves.

After dinner in the surprisingly comfortable inn, *El Presidente* took the opportunity to assemble the officers he had with him for a council of war. Having captured several talkative prisoners, and with more information from his active network of scouts and spies, he knew that Houston was somewhere near Groce's Plantation and that the rebel cabinet, at least some of it, probably was in Harrisburg, only 30 miles away from the river crossing at Fort Bend, which was a day's march from the inn if he pushed hard. Two days at most.

Assessing the situation on a map laid out on the long wood table where they had just dined, Santa Anna saw that with luck and speed he might be able to capture the entire rebel cabinet, then swing north to destroy Houston's army and finally bring this tiresome rebellion to an end. Sending word to General Sesma to move out immediately, the next morning Santa Anna resumed his march to the river with 750 men. True, it was a smaller force than he would have liked, but more than sufficient to crush anything in his path.

What Santa Anna and his staff didn't know was that the eager young man who always seemed to be hovering about as he served dinner, Mrs. Powell's son, Joseph, understood Spanish and listened intently to everything they said. No sooner was the cocksure Santa Anna out of sight the next morning than Joseph saddled the family mule and took off for Houston's camp with news of the Mexican plan, including troop dispositions and numbers.

Saddle sore and hungry, young Joseph rode into camp two days later with the news that Santa Anna was headed for Harrisburg with only 750 men, fewer men than in Houston's army. The general immediately sent out orders to his scattered troops, which included several patrols, plus the men led by Martin and Baker, to gather at the prosperous plantation owned by Charles Donoho.

———

HAVING the entire army gather on Donoho's property only seemed fair. The man was a notorious Tory, someone who had a good life under the Mexican government and saw no reason to change no matter how many of his neighbors suffered.

Politics was one thing, but the man was insufferable, too. When Houston rode up to the big house and attempted to assure the blustering landowner that his property and the property of all private citizens would be respected by the army, the obnoxious Donoho whined that Houston was too late.

"You great fool!" he practically shrieked, wagging his finger under Houston's nose. "This mob of barbarians you call an army have already damaged my property and land beyond repair, and here you are doing nothing about it."

When Houston patiently explained that he'd only just arrived and that Donoho would be compensated by the Texas government for any losses, the plantation owner laughed in his face.

"Everyone knows that motley collection of rascals doesn't have two pennies to rub together," sneered Donoho, who was of the well-fed, pink-cheeked sort that always seemed to rile Houston no matter where he found them. "Besides, when you're all dead or in a Mexican prison, who'll be left to pay for my time, trouble, and losses?"

Stifling the urge to seized Donoho by his lapels, throw him off his own veranda and kick him down the road, Houston turned on his heel and walked away, teeth grinding.

That night, Donoho was back again, this time complaining that the army was cutting down his trees for firewood.

Houston glanced at Hockley, who had reluctantly escorted Donoho into the tent.

"I'm afraid that's true, sir," the aide admitted. "The wood is awful green and they've had to cut down quite a few trees."

By now, the harried general had enough of this nonsense, but took pains not to show it. His face full of sympathy that he didn't feel, Houston rose to his feet and put his hand on the smaller Donoho's soft shoulder, guiding him out of the tent and into the open camp.

"Well, we certainly can't have that, can we, Mister Dono-ho," he said. "Hockley, tell the men that they can no longer cut down this man's trees for firewood. Pass the word that anyone who is caught will be severely disciplined."

Smiling at the mix of triumph and pleasure on Donoho's round face, Houston added, "I suggest that the men use his nice dry fence rails instead. As a matter of fact, they should use all of them, down to the last splinter."

A grinning Hockley snapped off a perfect salute, offered a crisp, "Yes, sir!" and ran off to give the delightful order.

Keeping a firm grip on the squirming Donoho's shoulder, Houston leaned over to whisper in his ear.

"And if you whine or complain even once more, I will have you tarred, feathered, and ridden out of camp on your last fence rail. Now get out of my sight, you fat oaf!"

15

COLONEL JUAN ALMONTE did not like this war and he did not like the way that *El Presidente* waged it.

They never should have bothered with San Antonio de Bejar. With most of the *Anglo* population concentrated well to the east, it is there that they should have attacked, not that isolated outpost in the west. A few swift strokes in the right place and the rebellion would have been crushed weeks ago.

But even assuming that the siege at Bejar was unavoidable – and no one except *El Presidente* thought so – if they had waited another day or two the siege cannon would have joined the army from the south and reduced the old mission to a pile of stones in just a few hours. But no, their leader had to have a great battle for his personal glory. As Santa Anna told his officers so many times, the lives of the men count for nothing. As it was, the useless victory at the Alamo and the dawdling with his new "bride" cost them 600 casualties and three weeks, a bit more than nothing.

The terrible slaughter of Fannin's men was another mistake. If Santa Anna had only let them go after a pledge to never again to raise arms against Mexico, word of his generosity would have spread and the rebellion fallen apart. Now the *Anglos* knew that there was no middle ground. It was either fight or die.

Dividing the army into so many separate commands was a preposterous idea, and a dangerous one. Instead of an over-whelming force that swept everything before it, the army was divided into what; three or four widely scattered parts, maybe more? Who could say? Plans changed so often that it was difficult to keep track of who was where and with how many men. Each of the segments was, if anything, all-too under-whelming, especially considering the condition of the men; tired, hungry and in poor health while Santa Anna lived soft and well with his silk tent, Persian slippers, and large collection of the finest wines.

Then there was the childish taunt that *El Presidente* demanded Almonte write in English and give to the captured ferryman at Fort Bend, who was released so he could hand it over to Houston. It was not only an action of almost breath-taking arrogance, it also told Houston of Santa Anna's plans and expectations. Almonte remembered every word: *"Mr. Houston: I know you are up there hiding in the bushes. As soon as I catch the other land thieves, I'm coming up there to smoke you out."* Such nonsense! Such vanity!

And this racing after a few miserable politicians was another absurdity. That scoundrel Houston and his armed rabble should be their target, not Burnet, de Zavala and the rest of the pathetic *Anglo* government, chosen by their peers as if they actually had a nation to govern. As Almonte knew from experience, most politicians are common and easily replaceable. This frenzied effort to run Burnet and his cabinet down was a diversion they did not need and could not afford. As long as Houston and his men remained in the field, the rebellion lived. It was that simple.

But Santa Anna was his president and his general and Juan

Almonte was a loyal man. Mexico had been in chaos ever since it declared its independence from Spain 15 years ago. The country needed a strong man to deliver it from that chaos and Santa Anna was a strong man, easily the most charismatic individual Almonte had ever met. True, *El Presidente* was not perfect. But who among us is?

As the illegitimate son of the revolutionary priest Jose Maria Morelos, Almonte recognized the irony of his support of a man who might become a dictator one day. One of the early leaders in the Mexican war for independence, Morelos was captured and executed when his son was only 12 years old. Educated in New Orleans, at only 20 years of age Almonte was a member of the Mexican delegation to London that negotiated a commercial treaty with the English, Mexico's first treaty as a new nation. By 27, he was a member of the Mexican congress and editor of *El Atleta*, a powerful newspaper that was savage in its criticism of President Anastasio Bustamente. When Bustamente ordered his arrest, Almonte was forced to flee to New Orleans. But such were the rapidly changing times and alliances that Bustamente brought him back so that Almonte could represent Mexico to Brazil and the various new South American republics.

Then, just two years ago, Almonte suddenly was ordered home and assigned to make a long inspection tour of *Tejas* and report what he witnessed. The widely-quoted report was straightforward and the conclusion was simple: Mexico would lose its northernmost province to the *Anglos* if it didn't take action quickly, stem the tide of *Norte Americano* immigration, and bring the immigrants to heel. After less than 20 years of easy immigration policy, the *Anglos* outnumbered the Mexicans in *Tejas* by 10 to 1. Although virtually all of them took the oath to become Mexican citizens, which was required to own land, most of them sneered at Mexican customs and ignored Mexican laws. If events continued as they were, Almonte concluded that within a few years *Tejas* would either become an independent nation, or part of the United States. Neither option was palatable to Mexico, whoever was in power. Nor should it be.

When Santa became *El Presidente* he immediately appointed Almonte, a man experienced beyond his years, as his aide de camp, someone who could do anything and did everything.

And now, here he was, in charge of 50 dragoons chasing a few bedraggled rebel politicians no one cared about except Santa Anna, who seemed to hold them in higher regard than the *Anglos* themselves.

———

As THEY CLOSED in on the Galveston Bay town of New Washington, one of Almonte's outriders galloped back to the main body to report that there was an *Anglo* courier riding just ahead. Almonte didn't bother to ask how the man knew it was a courier. He was too reliable to be doubted.

"Good, perhaps he will finally lead us to Burnet and the cabinet," he told the scout. "Take three men and follow him, but don't let him see you. We will be behind you at a safe distance. When you are sure about the courier's destination, send a message and we will move up quickly."

The lone rider was, in fact, a courier. Young Mike McCormick, whose mother, a 49-year-old Irish spitfire named Peggy McCormick, owned a ranch that was ideally situated on the fertile land between the San Jacinto River and San Jacinto Bay, carried dispatches for President Burnet, who was supposed to be just ahead at New Washington.

Twenty minutes earlier, a gentle nicker from a Mexican horse gave the enemy away. An expert horseman who was raised in Texas and wise beyond his years, from what he heard McCormick knew that a large Mexican patrol was nearby. He felt the presence of too many horses for it to be anything else. The Texian army was too far away. It hadn't send patrols in this direction in weeks.

In case President Burnet really was up ahead, McCormick needed to warn the president before the Mexicans moved in on the town, which was mostly a collection of warehouses to store the shipping traffic. The timing was critical. It took all of the young man's self control to continue his casual lope into town while praying that the Mexicans wouldn't make their charge before he gave warning.

As he approached the water end of one of the warehouses, McCormick spotted Burnet, who'd often stayed at their ranch, his wife, Hannah, and two of their brats. Deciding that he'd waited long enough, he spurred his horse to a run, waved his hat, and shouted, "Run for your lives! The Mexicans are coming! The Mexicans are coming!"

With his friend, Dr. George Patrick, Burnet was on a dock overseeing the loading of a large skiff with trunks containing his personal items, plus some official government papers. Reacting quickly to McCormick's warning, he ordered his indentured servant to bring the boat around to the beach so his wife and children could board easily. Burnet scooped up one of his children while Patrick picked up the other. They dumped them in the skiff and then helped Burnet's wife aboard. David Thomas, who was Secretary of War now that Rusk had joined Houston's army, jumped into a flatboat with several other men, all of them scrambling to launch, which they finally did with two muscular blacks pulling at the oars. At the same time, seeing the President's party respond to his warning, McCormick wheeled his horse and dashed for safety into the woods.

In a ragged charge, Almonte's dragoons thundered down the grassy hill to the shoreline, where they quickly dismounted and primed their rifles. Burnet, Patrick, and Burnet's indentured servant pulled hard at the skiff's oars in a hopeless attempt to get out of range. Seeing that they'd never make it, Burnet dropped his oar and awkwardly stood in the skiff as it rocked back and forth, partially screening his wife and children and offering himself as a target.

With the President of Texas presenting himself as an easy target no more than 50 yards away, Almonte nodded his assent and his second in command took control of the line of riflemen, who were all down on one knee and ready to fire.

"*Listo! Objectivo! Fue ...!*"

"*ALTO! ALTO!*" Almonte bellowed just as the men were about pull their triggers.

Rifles drooping, the surprised dragoons looked at their colonel as if he had lost his mind.

"There is a woman in the boat," he explained, looking intently at the skiff. "Children, too. I think."

The men peered at the skiff, which was still in easy range. Yes, they could see a woman crouching behind the still upright Burnet. There was at least one *nino*, too.

"I do not make war against women and children," Almonte said, as much to himself as to his men. "No miserable politician's life is worth that."

16

THE ARMY WAS on the move again. At the front of the long ragged line, Houston and Rusk rode side by side, their stirrups almost touching each other on the narrow road out of Donoho's, which, to Houston's satisfaction, did not have a fence, or even a fence rail, in sight.

Although a storm passed through overnight, the sun was out and the rain had cleared the air so that everything seemed fresh, new and alive. For the first time in weeks there was no immediate crisis for Houston to fret about. There were plenty of things he *could* have worried about, but for now it felt good to be on the move again and feel the sun's warmth on his face while he enjoyed the spirited gait of his new horse, a white stallion named Saracen. With all that to give him pleasure, he took a deep breath and savored the moment because he knew that the immediate future wouldn't hold many like it.

"It's a fine day, or promises to be such," observed Rusk,

who, from his jaunty attitude, looked like he was feeling equally lighthearted.

"So, general, you know *my* story," Rusk continued, speaking in the familiar way they'd adopted since that day Rusk joined the army. "How I came to Texas lookin' for those damn thieves who stole all the money I invested in the mining company, and then decided to stay on. But what about you? There's all manner of wild rumors out there, which I'm sure you already know. But if you don't mind my askin', what really brought you to Texas?"

Suddenly the fine day took on a gray cast as the world seemed to darken with Houston's mood.

It wasn't as if he was never asked the question. In the more than three years since he'd crossed the border into Texas from the north, splashing across a shallow stretch of the Red River on a sleek broom-tailed mare, the subject came up more often than he liked, though less so these last few months with so much else to worry about. Those who asked didn't really want to know why he came to Texas. They wanted to know what happened before that. They wanted to know about the great catastrophes of his life. Some of it they already knew, or thought they knew, but they wanted him to tell it for their entertainment, as if he somehow owed it to them.

They wanted to know why he so suddenly resigned as governor of Tennessee, forsaking the brightest political future in the land, one that might even have led to the presidency.

They wanted to know about his brief and terrible marriage to Eliza Allen that started his stunning downfall.

They wanted to know what really happened when he left Tennessee to live with the Cherokee up in Indian territory. Did he really marry a Cherokee woman without bothering to divorce Eliza? Was it really true that he was dead drunk for most of those years, and that it got so bad he was known to the Cherokee as Big Drunk?

Did he really beat a congressman senseless on the streets of Washington, D.C., for insults spoken in the House of Representatives?

And was it true that he came to Texas as President Jackson's private agent, with the clear and illegal intention of somehow breaking Texas away from Mexico?

Though most were too polite to say so directly, they wanted to know all of those things and more.

And so far, Sam Houston refused to tell them. He intended to keep on not telling them, too. Why should he? It was none of their damn business. Let them all accept him as he was or not at all.

At least that is what he told himself. The truth was something different; much different. He knew it, too.

He would not talk about what passed between them because after almost seven years it was still too raw and humiliating. He would not reveal that she was cold to him from the first night of their doomed marriage. He would not tell of his mad alcohol-sparked jealously that drove her away after only a few weeks. He would not speak of her savage scorn that cut him raw and the final quarrel that saw him nearly kill her father. He would tell no one of these things. He would not bother to deny the fantastic rumors that rose out of the public scandal that led to his resignation as governor and the fateful decision to leave Tennessee and go west to join the same band of Cherokee he lived with as a boy. Why did he do it? Because he had no where else to go.

While he would not speak of Eliza, he *could* not speak of Tiana, his beloved Cherokee bride who sustained and supported him when no one else would. He could not tell anyone how he became little more than a helpless, self-pitying drunk, and how he deserted her at their sad little trading post and traveled to Washington, desperate to start his life anew, if only he could find a second chance after squandering the first.

He could not speak of her because the thought of Tiana tore at his heart until the terrible pain made him cry out at night. There were times when he thought that it might kill him, knowing that he left her because he was a coward. She deserved everything and he gave her nothing. He could not bear the thought of what he did to her, not yet and maybe not ever.

So no, he would not speak of these things and damn anyone who asked.

Giving Rusk a level, dead-eyed stare, Houston spoke more formally than he ever had to the man.

"Colonel Rusk, you will remain at the head of the column until you receive further orders. I will ride back and inspect the line of march."

Houston pulled hard on his reins and wheeled Saracen, who responded eagerly to the command, and galloped back down the long snaking line of marching men, ignoring their friendly waves and hails.

Behind him, Tom Rusk wished he'd kept his big mouth shut. He'd never seen such an instant flash of raw anger on another man's face. His regret was interrupted when Hockley galloped up and eased his horse to Rusk's side. In the few weeks they'd known each other, the men had become good friends.

"What the hell happened, Tom? Even from back where I was, it looked like the general was hit by a lightning bolt."

Rusk explained the brief conversation.

"Oh, my God!" Holding the reins in one hand, Hockley took off his hat and ran his forearm across his brow. "I should have warned you back when you first got here. I'm surprised he didn't pull a pistol and threaten to blow your fool head off. I've seen him do it. Worse things, too."

"What worse things," asked Rusk?

"My friend, you don't want to know," Hockley said. "I'm

just glad there's no alcohol around here for the general to find."

That surprised Rusk. "You mean there's no liquor anywhere in this army?"

"Of course, there is," Hockley admitted. "What I mean is that the general doesn't have any by his own order and he's too proud to go around askin' for it."

THAT NIGHT, he felt the melancholy coming on again. He knew the signs all too well, but most of the time he couldn't do anything about it. Whenever it took hold, it seemed to beat him down until he felt crushed from his own despair. But this time he couldn't give into it. He had too many enemies who were waiting for him to fail; who *expected* him to fail so they could pounce and bring him down. It would only confirm what they already thought.

And if he fell apart now, who would command the army? There was no one else. It wasn't just his vanity talking, although he knew that he had had plenty of vanity. No, it was simple fact, at least as he saw it. He was the only one who could keep everything together and moving forward. Without momentum, the revolution would die. Others may not see that, but he did.

So he could not give in. He must not give in. Work was the answer. It almost always was; anything to divert his heart and mind from the awful abyss.

And then he found it. The six-pound cannon from Cincinnati had finally arrived – someone called them the Twin Sisters and the name stuck – and now they needed crews and someone to command them. As he expected, the cannon were such morale boosters that when the call went out for volunteers no fewer than forty men offered their services, although only nine per cannon were needed. Karnes scoffed that artillery duty drew so many eager volunteers because cannon worked at a distance. The worst fighting was always close in.

While Karnes had a point, Houston knew that the Twin Sisters would be valuable in the campaign, especially against Santa Anna's cavalry, which were more numerous and better than anything they had. He decided to stop sulking – easier said than done, he knew - and take a closer look at the newest addition to his army. It was a good idea to become familiar with the Twin Sister's capabilities, too. It had been a while since he was around cannon of any size.

He nodded to the guard as he approached the cannon, moving close to touch them here and there with his big hands. He always liked getting the feel of things that way. The six-pound cannon were smoothbore, meaning that the insides of their barrels were not rifled, which cut down on their long-range accuracy. In a perfect world, cannon such as these fired cast-iron balls, but the army had precious few of those, probably no more than a half-dozen. To make more cannon balls, the gun crews would have to make do with any melted-down metal they could find, anything from candlesticks to discarded horseshoes and broken bayonets.

In addition to the solid shot, the Twin Sisters fired smaller round shot such as canister or grapeshot. Grapeshot was usually packed in a tightly wrapped cloth rag, which gave the appearance of clusters of grapes. Both canister and grapeshot scattered after being fired from the barrel and were mostly useful at close range, like a giant shotgun, where the carnage could be terrible.

He raked his memory to recall the many skills needed to handle the guns, a unique mix of expertise and muscle that required at least seven trained men, including gunners, loaders, spongers, and powder monkeys, usually youngsters who were strong enough to keep the power coming and nimble enough to stay out of the way. The sponger used a long wood cylinder, covered on one end with lambskin, which was dipped in water and inserted into the barrel. The sponge quenched any sparks left from the previous shot and was twisted in the barrel to clean it of gunpowder residue so that the cannon wouldn't explode and maim or kill the men working it. Once the barrel was clean, a black powder cartridge was rammed into the barrel by a long-handled rammer and compressed with a clump of cotton rags known as the wad. That was followed by the projectile, which had to be free of dirt so it wouldn't jam the barrel and low it to pieces. A six-pound ball usually took the same amount of power. More powder was poured into the vent at the rear of the cannon, known as the touchhole, and another man shoved a pick down the vent that pierced the cartridge to ensure that it would ignite. Finally, the artillery officer put a burning match on the touchhole with a long stock called a limstock, which finally fired the cannon

All of that was well and good. The men could be found. He was sure of it. There were plenty to choose from. But who did he have to command? As always, that was the key.

Looking around to make sure there was no gunpowder nearby, Houston crossed his long legs and leaned against one of the Twin Sister's big wheels while he stoked up a cigar. To better transport the things, in the morning he'd order them taken apart, with the barrels and wheels separated and carried by pack animals. Come the time, they'd be easy enough to reassemble with a few minutes warning.

But who to command?

Then it came to him - Jim Neill!

James Clinton Neill was the perfect choice in every way Houston could think of. Two or three years older than Houston, the veteran lieutenant colonel was a man whose word carried weight, someone other men would obey. Like several others in the army, including Houston himself, Neill was at Horseshoe Bend with Jackson. With his wife and three children, he came to Texas two years before Houston. If the stories were true, it was Neill who fired the first shot of the revolution from the famous "Come and Take It" cannon at Gonzales.

Back in December, Neill commanded the cannon when Stephen Austin's men took Bejar from General Martin Cos and his garrison, though everybody knew that it was old Ben Milam, and not Austin, who was the guiding spirit of the assault. Unfortunately, Milam was killed by a sniper during the siege. Sickly as he was, the monk-like Austin had his uses, but he was no military man.

With Cos' surrender, Neill took command of the small garrison left at Bejar. When Houston asked for a report summarizing the defenses, the commander's words were gloomy. The place was undermanned and under-supplied, he complained, with fewer than a hundred unpaid men dressed in rags and near starvation. Houston remembered Neill's plaintive whine: "If there has ever been a dollar here I have no knowledge of it." When Houston ordered that the Alamo's twenty cannon be hauled to safety, Neill bluntly replied that it was impossible because he had no draft animals with which to do it.

Houston sent Bowie to Bejar, then Travis showed up, and suddenly things changed, much against Houston's wishes. Instead of getting out, as Houston wanted, they choose to stand and fight. Houston realized now than Jim Bowie was the wrong man to order to run from anything. Somewhere in his trunk of papers, he still had Bowie's letter praising Neill: "No other man in the army could have kept the men at this post, under the neglect they have experienced." Bowie did not say such a thing unless he meant it.

On February 11, less than two weeks before the siege

began, Neill learned that his wife and children were seriously ill. Frantic with worry, he left Bejar to be with his family. Although the children survived, his wife died. Houston didn't know for sure, but he figured that it had to be typhoid. It was the only thing he knew of that moved that fast, the same thing that killed Bowies' young wife and her parents. Despite the tragedy, the dutiful Neill was headed back to Bejar with 48 men when they were forced to turn back by Mexican patrols. The Alamo had fallen.

After that, something changed in the man. While there were no whispers of cowardice that Houston ever heard, it was as if Neill was afraid that there might be, or that someone was saying it behind his back. It was as if he regretted not staying at the Alamo and dying with the rest of them. Or maybe it had to do with the death of his wife? Neill never talked about it – Houston, of all men, could understand that - and there was no way to know. But Jim Neill was not the same man. There was a kind of uncertainty to him now, as if he was going through the motions for lack of anything better to do. At the same time, he seemed defensive and quarrelsome, often seeing insults where none were intended. He was a man adrift. Houston thought. Perhaps the responsibility of a new and important command might restore his spirit? There was only one way to find out.

Having made his decision, with a final nod to the guard at the Twin Sisters, Houston tossed the cigar aside started back to his tent, chuckling that the guard probably was relieved to see him go. The man obviously was puzzled at his general's strange behavior as he walked around the cannon, ran his hands across one or the other from time to time, and muttered to himself.

Being led by a crazy man probably didn't inspire much confidence.

17

To my darling wife,

I can only hope that this simple hastily-written missive reaches you in timely fashion. I fear that the mail is much disrupted by the rebellion, as is any form of communication, so much so that in many areas it has ceased to exist. I hurriedly scribble these few lines so that they will be ready when a courier leaves within the hour.

I hope that the tumultuous times find you in fine health and good spirits. You may rest assured that I am quite safe. The part of the army in which I serve has seen no fighting as yet so I have been at no risk whatsoever. However, I know that benign situation will not last forever and I am eager to do my part when the time comes. It is my dearest hope to make you proud.

We did have a rare treat this afternoon. Our redoubtable scouts, Henry Karnes and Deaf Smith, somehow captured an enemy wagon full of flour in barrels. When the duo rode into camp with the wagon, I was among the fortunate men nearby who received a portion of the flour, a much appreciated change from our usual fare of half-cooked beef and ground corn. In order to do something palatable with it, a group of us went to a nearby creek, washed our dirty handkerchiefs as best we could and mixed the dough in them. We then fashioned sticks about the size of a man's wrist, wrapped the dough around the sticks, and held our creation over the fire until it was well browned. I do believe that I have never eaten anything so delicious in all my life. As I write this, my stomach still is pleasantly full and I am near overcome by a sense of well being. Such is the salubrious effect of a full stomach.

Although we still are our in our mode of near-constant retreat, our morale, at least among the rank and file, remains remarkably high. I hope you are not disappointed that I still am among the rank and file. It is by my own choice. I have twice been put up for promotion and refused it both times. My utter lack of experience in military affairs makes me eager to avoid the responsibility of promotion and command. Too, I find my companions to be such stout and agreeable fellows that I am loath to be placed above them.

In all fairness, I should tell you of a curious division within the army that leads to near-constant friction. Many of the officers grumble and criticize constantly in ways that seem to me to fall just short of mutinous, while most of the men, both militia and regular army, have a deep respect for and trust in General Houston. The general must be aware the constant sniping from so many of his officers and yet, as far as I can see, he simply ignores it.

To illustrate warmth and camaraderie with which most of us regard him, I will tell you of a splendid joke played on the general by some few of the men. It came as a result of an incident several weeks ago when General Houston took the time to personally repair a private's rifle, which revealed the general's impressive skill in that area, one that none of us suspecte that he possessed.

A recruit who joined us just the day before came into camp complaining that his weapon – an aged revolutionary war-era

*Kentucky rifle – was broken and asked if there was a black-
smith traveling with the army who might repair it. At that time,
there was only one erect tent in camp and that belonged to
General Houston. Several of the lighter spirits - I blush to
disclose that I was among them - informed the young man that
the tent was, in fact, the blacksmith's quarters and the tall,
powerful looking man standing outside the tent at that moment
was the blacksmith. The recruit boldly walked up to the "blacksmith," who was, as I am sure you have guessed by now, General
Houston himself, and asked him to fix his rifle right away.*

*Instead of exploding in anger, as many of us expected, the
general meekly replied that he would take a look at the weapon.
If it could be fixed, he promised to return it as soon as possible.
If you find that odd, I am sure that General Houston realized
that he was the victim of a prank and decided to play along.*

*As soon as the man left, in full view of us all General
Houston took the lock off the weapon, cleaned it, and reassem-
bled it. The news quickly spread all over the army, of course,
and we waited to see what would happen next, without trying to
be too obvious about it and give the game away.*

*In the meantime, someone told the unfortunate owner of the
gun that he had presented his aged weapon to none other than
the general himself and that there was a rumor in the camp that
the hot-tempered general intended to have him shot for giving
such an insult. The poor fellow was nearly out of his wits and
asked everyone he met, "What shall I do? Oh, God, what shall I
do? They told me he was a blacksmith. How was I to know?"*

*Finally, we suggested that the best thing was to go to the
general and beg forgiveness. If he did that, perhaps he would
only be court-martialed and not executed. So he went, and with
hat in hand tremblingly told his story.*

*General Houston said, 'My friend, they told you right. I am
a very good blacksmith.' Taking up the gun, he snapped the
mechanism two or three times. 'She is in good order now and I*

hope that you'll do some good with it.' I have never seen such relief as I saw on the recruits' face, the poor fellow. Admittedly, it was a cruel jest, but such is the rough humor of army life.

With such spirit in this army, how can we not prevail despite all the nay sayers and malcontents who complain without offering solution?

I see the courier saddling his horse, so I will end this letter on that positive note. I promise that I will write again as soon as I can.

>*Your devoted husband,*
>*Daniel*

18

"GENERAL, have you met the new man?" asked Hockley, standing to one side in the tent while Houston looked into a shard from a broken mirror that he held with his left hand while carefully shaving with his right.

"What new man," asked Houston absently, which Hockley took to mean that he had not?

"It's a gentleman from Georgia. His name's Lamar, Mirabeau Buonaparte Lamar."

"His name is what?"

Houston put the shard of mirror on his camp stool, grabbed a dirty shirt and wiped his face dry. Because he only shaved once a week at most these days, he enjoyed it when he did and tended to linger over the process. But there was something in Hockley's manner that made him cut it short; something insistent, but hesitant at the same time. It was as if he had something to say but didn't know how to go about it.

"Yes, sir, Mirabeau Buonaparte Lamar, recently arrived from Georgia," Hockley repeated, nervously shifting his weight from one foot to the other.

"Now that's a two-dollar name," Houston said with a smile.

"It must play hell when he has to affix his signature to something or other. Why do you ask if I met him particularly? Why this Lamar and not some other new man? Talk to me, Hockley, and stop fidgeting like a school boy who doesn't know his lessons."

"It ... it's just that ... there's something about him ...."

"Hockley, I am no longer young. I don't have time to stand here and listen to you stammer. Out with it, man! Say your piece. I promise not to interrupt."

"Well, sir, he came into camp with several other volunteers. I'm told that he fancies himself an artist. He's a painter and a poet, too, and even published a newspaper for a while. He's thirty eight and they say he came to Texas with at least six thousand dollars to invest in land for a Georgia syndicate."

"Get rid of the poetry, change the numbers a bit, and you've described more than a few of the men in this army," Houston said. "What's so special about this man that makes you so eager to tell me about him? And I do apologize for the interruption. Now go on with whatever the hell you're talkin' about."

"There's something about him, sir. They say he's a natural leader, the kind of man other men listen to and maybe even follow."

"Are you suggestin' that I should promote him already?"

Hockley vigorously shook his head. "No, sir, not at all. Quite the opposite, in fact."

The aide took a deep breath, embarrassed at how he was babbling, but needing to protect his general no matter how foolish he looked.

"He claims that he only wants to be a private and nothin' more. But he stopped a while in Harrisburg on the way here and I understand that he's already part of the Burnet faction."

"You mean that faction which takes the position that I am

a damned incompetent fool who is better suited to cleaning privies than leading armies?"

Although Houston captured it exactly, for once Hockley thought it best not to agree with his general and kept talking, hurrying to say what he needed to say before he embarrassed himself any more than he already had.

"Well, sir, Lamar's come up with some scheme to use the Yellowstone, which, as you know, is docked at Groce's Landing, to raid the Mexican positions downriver. The problem is that some of the men are starting to listen, especially those who think we're retreated too far for too long. Lamar's a good talker and a persuasive man, but without seeming to try to persuade anybody about anything. He hasn't said anything specifically against you, but somehow everything he says is against you, if you know what I mean."

"So this Mirabeau Bounaparte Lamar wants to divert men to the fundamentally stupid idea of using that leaky little steamboat to attack the Mexicans as if it was a mighty flotilla," asked Houston?

"I'm sure he doesn't put it that way, but, yes, that's the gist of it, sir. And this steamboat notion is just one idea. He's already voiced several others. I think mostly he wants to rally the men to himself and march off to glory."

"Does he, indeed?" Houston stood for a moment as if lost in thought. "Thank you, Hockley. And I do apologize for my earlier sarcasm. Sometimes I can't help myself. You were quite correct to inform me about this man. Never hesitate to approach me with your concerns, son. It's rare that I will criticize a man who takes the initiative, unless it's against orders. I have always believed that it's better to do something and be wrong than to do nothing and regret it later, though it's landed me in trouble more than a time or two. I'd say Mirabeau Buonaparte Lamar seems to be of the same mind."

When Hockley left, relieved that the clumsy conversation

was over at last, Houston smiled to himself. He already knew a few things about Lamar. He'd been warned about the newcomer by a letter from Vice President de Zavala. As he told Tom Rusk a while back, de Zavala was *not* one of his informants in Burnet's cabinet, but the vice president felt that Lamar was someone he needed to be informed about. He was happy to hear Hockley's assessment, too. His aide was a canny observer who usually saw more in a glance than most men did in several days of serious study. And Houston hadn't heard about the ridiculous Yellowstone plot. What dangerous nonsense!

Before leaving Harrisburg to join the army, Lamar wrote to his brother, Jefferson J. Lamar, back in Macon, Georgia. De Zavala happened to see the letter - for a man who claimed to be too ethical to spy de Zavala seemed awfully good at it - and passed the contents on to Houston:

"A dreadful battle is to be fought in three or four days on the Brazos, decisive of the fate of Texas. (Really, thought Houston? Three or four days? Being the general, you'd think I'd know.) *I shall of course have to be in it.* (Well, of course, agreed Houston. I believe that I can arrange it, too.) *Texas is in a dreadful state of confusion.* (When is it not?) *The Mexicans thus far are prevailing. San Antonio has been taken by them and every man in the fort murdered.* (True enough, agreed Houston, though I wonder why Goliad didn't rate a mention. The poet in Lamar probably didn't find it sufficiently heroic.)

As Hockley said, Lamar's letter managed to be inoffensive and near insubordinate at the same time. This man promised to be an interesting opponent. Potentially useful, too. Perhaps even a fit rival for Houston's other rivals. Divide and conquer? Not a bad idea.

But whatever he did about Lamar, it was time to put his foot down again. Some of the men and officers were feeling a bit too frisky. A few days ago, a number of volunteers got together and "officially" nominated Sidney Sherman as the best man to lead them. Houston didn't know if that meant just the volunteers, or the entire army. Probably they weren't sure either. Even if they were just blowing off a little steam, he couldn't let it go any further.

He sat at his portable desk and thought a bit. Then he began to write, the pen flying across the page. After a few minutes, he summoned Hockley.

"I want a detail to dig graves," Houston said.

"Graves, sir?"

"Yes. Two will suffice. Dig them beneath a tree as close to the center of camp as you can find." He handed Hockley what he'd written. "Once the graves are dug, post this on the tree. Have someone you trust linger nearby. Your presence would be too obvious. When Lamar reads it, as I am sure he will, tell me, and then inform him that I want to see him right away. Understand?"

Hockley read Houston's words and a broad grin spread across his face.

"Yes, sir." Hockley turned to go, but stopped at the tent entrance. "And if I may say so ...."

"No, you may not say so. This kind of thing has to be done sometimes, but I find it distasteful. There'll be no crowing about it. We spend too much time squabbling with each other."

The notice over the graves was brief and to the point. It declared that anyone who attempted to "beat for volunteers" and undertake an unauthorized mission of any kind would be shot. Further, any other mutinous talk or action would immediately result in court martial and execution.

Houston still doubted that he had it within himself to order an execution. He just wasn't that cold-blooded. Fortunately, the men didn't know it.

Lamar entered the tent about 90 minutes later. Houston

pretended to be busy with paperwork. When he looked up, he saw a man of medium height, with a square face, alert blue eyes, and dark hair hanging down to his collar.

He also appeared to have a built-in smirk, no doubt one of those who thought they were smarter than everyone else around them, which was, in fact, was often the case with such men. Houston knew the type well. As a younger man, he'd often seen it back at the Hermitage, Andrews Jackson's plantation and great house outside of Nashville. Some men had the faculty of saying the best and most clever things so that they were often quoted for days or weeks afterward. But at the same time they gave the impression that they had much better in reserve if they really cared to produce it. Even standing in silence, Lamar gave exactly that impression.

Fair enough, thought Houston. If this Hotspur fights as well as they say that he talks then he may be useful in ways that he can't imagine. I believe that I will set him against Sherman and see what happens. It just might serve them both right.

Houston stood and introduced himself, his big hand engulfing Lamar's. In the small tent, Houston's height and bulk dwarfed everything about Lamar, which was exactly his intention.

"Please, take a seat," he said, motioning to the cot. There was only one way for a man to sit on the edge of a cot while being interviewed by his general for the first time and that was awkwardly. Lamar was already uncomfortable. Good.

"I've heard about you, yes, I have, indeed," Houston saw a flicker of uncertainty in the Georgian's large blue eyes. He wasn't sure why he was summoned to the general's tent, but after the posted notice he feared the worst. "You are a man of action, I believe."

They talked a bit, things of no consequence. Houston watched while Lamar tried not to squirm, generally doing a fine job of it. He was good, but not quite good enough. No man of intrigue liked to be caught so early in the game, or at all.

"Lamar, how would you feel about assignment to the cavalry," Houston asked? "You'd serve under Lieutenant Colonel Sherman, of course. I have a notion that you two will get along – oh, what's the word? - *famously*."

"I would be honored, General Houston," Lamar replied in a soft Georgia drawl with considerable relief in it. "A privilege, in fact."

"I was hoping you'd say that," agreed Houston. "A prudent decision, if I say so myself."

19

EVEN THOUGH IT was months ago, Granville Kirkup remembered the advice as clearly as he remembered the bad camp coffee and corn mush he forced down this morning.

It came from Nicholas Yoakum, two days before he was killed in the courtyard of the Veramendi palace when they took Bejar back in December. Yoakum was done in by the same sniper who shot Ben Milam in the head a few minutes later. Kirkup was one of the marksmen who replied with a vengeance and blew that Mexican out of the tree from where he did so much damage.

"Granville, if you want to get out of this war alive, then find a way to hook up with that feller over there." Yoakum nodded toward a man who was sharpening his Bowie knife in the shade of a scraggly tree in the camp outside of Bejar.

"His name's Erastus Smith, but everybody calls him Deaf," Yoakum continued, pronouncing the name "Deef." "He just may be the smartest man in this fight and you would be wise to stay with him like a tick on an old dog. You might even get to like him, assuming he lets you stick close enough."

At first, Kirkup thought that Yoakum had pointed out the

wrong man. Deaf Smith was a gnarled old character, all weather beaten and lumpy. A little above middling height, with hair that was as gray as it was thinning, to someone as young as the 20 year old Kirkup he looked like he must be a hundred years old.

That was only four months ago but it seemed like just short of forever. Taking Yoakum's advice, Kirkup made a point of following Smith like a faithful puppy. Where Smith went, he went, until he was eventually accepted as one of Smith's small group of scouts. Being English born and only one year in Texas, Kirkup knew that he was the least skillful of Smith's men, although he was one of the best shots in the army. But he was learning fast and being one of that select group raised him higher in the esteem of most of the rest of the men. While it was true that Kirkup was still very much alive, as Yoakum predicted - and convinced that Smith was some kind of genius, in his peculiar way - the young Englishman had more close scrapes in a few months than most men have in their whole lives.

And now they were at it again.

"Boy, you're comin' with me," Smith ordered, kicking Kirkup out of a pleasant early morning sleep. "Boy" was all that Smith and the rest of the scouts ever called him. It was never Granville, or Gran, or even Kirkup; just "Boy."

Tying his roll behind his saddle in case they were gone over night, Kirkup asked, "Where are we headed?" He remembered to look directly at Smith as he spoke. Otherwise the older man couldn't hear a thing, though Kirkup suspected that he could read lips.

"You and me are goin' on a scout," Smith replied, swinging one leg over the saddle as he mounted the sorry looking little mare he favored because it was blistering fast over short distances and had no end of endurance when endurance was needed. "What's your fancy English word for it, a rec-oh ...?"

"A reconnoiter?"" suggested Kirkup.

As they rode out of camp, Smith laughed. "Yes, we are going on a proper reconnoiter. The general wants to know how many Mexican's are closest, who's leadin' 'em, where they are, and where they're goin'. I reckon he figures that if everything falls together for us somethin' might break loose soon."

After more than a day and a half in the saddle - Smith insisted that whenever possible all his men dismount and walk 10 minutes our of every hour to relieve the mounts - judging by the noise and dust coming over a hill to the south they found what they were looking for.

"There's nobody else except us and the Mexicans with that many men to make such a sign," Smith muttered. "And nobody but the Mexicans wouldn't bother with outriders. We should never have gotten this close without bein' seen. Pretty sure of themselves, ain't they?"

Smith tugged on the reins and kicked his little horse into a trot, intending to work their way around behind the Mexican force.

"C'mon, boy. We'll get to their rear and follow 'em," he explained. "They like to stop early so there should be plenty of daylight left for a look see. The country bein' what it is, we'll probably have to do it out in the open. Hope you don't scare easy."

As usual, Smith was right. There were several hours of daylight left when the Mexicans stopped for the day. Smith took the lead as they approached the camp from the rear until they were on a rise about 400 yards away. The veteran scout pulled out an old telescope from his saddlebag and methodically began counting flags so he could give accurate numbers to Houston.

"You see that big blue-and-white stripped tent they're puttin' up in the center of camp," Smith asked, jerking his chin forward to point? "That's Santa Anna himself. His tent's bigger'n most cabins I've seen. Made of silk, too. Walked right by it a few times. One time, *El Presidente* ordered me to light his *cigarro* for him."

"What did you do?"

"I lit his *cigarro*. Didn't have much choice."

Kirkup had heard the stories but until now found them hard to believe. With his deep tan, slim stature, and intimate knowledge of the Mexican language and culture, after changing into Mexican clothing and gear Smith sometimes boldly rode into the enemy camp, where he gathered information through idle conversation and keen-eyed observance. When he finished, he simply rode away. Kirkup could not imagine such a thing. The man must have no nerves at all.

As Smith continued his silent count, he explained that the flags represented different units in the Mexican army. If you knew which flags represented which units, and how many men were in those units, then it was easy to calculate the overall number. All you had to do was get close enough.

Which had turned into a pressing problem, in Kirkup's view. He watched nervously as a company of infantry marched out of the Mexican camp from the left, headed in their direction. About 150 yards away, the infantry stopped, lined up, saw to their weapons, and began firing. Musket balls whistled all around them, some hitting the ground at their horses' feet while others zipped past dangerously close to Kirkup's ears. While the shooting made his horse skitter back and forth with nervousness, Smith's disciplined little mount stood statue still, allowing its oblivious rider to continue his placid count.

After 10 minutes that seemed like an eternity - a musket ball struck Kirkup's saddle horn and blew it to pieces; he had to bite his lip to keep from yelping - the Mexicans sent out a squadron of dragoons to drive the pests away.

As the riders approached, Smith ceased his counting and turned to Kirkup. "I think them fellers want to shoo us away. Time to git," he said, putting spur to horse.

Only then did Kirkup realize that Smith never heard any of the shots fired at them. It was only the dragoons that got his attention.

As he explained later in camp, to the amusement of every man listening, "I never obeyed an order more cheerfully."

———

HE NEVER LIKED BEING CALLED "DEAF" Smith, though nobody knew it, not even his wife Guadalupe and their four daughters. He didn't protest because there was nothing he could do. Even the Mexicans called him *"El Sordo,"* the deaf.

Smith knew that they didn't mean anything by it, but that didn't mean he had to like it. That was one of the things he admired about the general. Right from the beginning, even before Houston took command of the army, he was always Erastus or Mister E, never Deaf. A proud man himself, Houston knew about the pride of other men.

And maybe there were compensations. He could see better than most anyone, but it was more than that. He had a way of sensing things, anything from people to animals. Danger, too. If there was something wrong in a situation, Smith usually knew it before anyone else. It was as if an apologetic nature tried to make up for taking his hearing away. It was a poor trade, but at least he got something in return.

And it could be worse. He knew that, too. Look at that man Williamson, who rode with the cavalry under Sidney Sherman. With that wooden leg he wore thanks to the way one leg was bent backwards by some childhood sickness, Robert Williamson, a lawyer and educated man, was known to everyone as "Three-Legged Willie." If the name bothered him, he gave no sign of it. But then, neither did Smith. From the time he lost his hearing as a boy, he vowed never to let them see it.

Despite what people thought, he was not a natural fighting man. He tried to stay out of the revolution at first, content in his family's little house at the corner of *Presa* and *Nueva* streets in Bejar. Who governed what didn't seem to matter much in those days, not to Smith and not to most of the people he knew. He had big plans after introducing a fine stock of Muley cattle from Louisiana on some land he had outside of Bejar, near the San Jose mission. It's true that he was fast closing in on 50, but he still had time to accomplish a few things. A man was only as old as he felt. The problem was that you never knew what you'd start feeling it.

Smith tended to agree when one of his neighbors, who didn't cotton to the revolution either, said that he didn't see why he should exchange one dictator five hundred miles away for five hundred dictators one mile away. The Mexicans always treated him well and he liked them in return. Hell, he even married one. As did most Texians, years ago he took the pledge to become a Mexican citizen and saw no reason to break it.

Smith was away on a hunting trip with his son-in-law, Hendrick Arnold, when Austin's motley excuse for an army started the siege at Bejar. Even with that, he figured that they wouldn't have any trouble getting back into town. Everybody knew that he was neutral in the fight. But a pompous Mexican officer commanding a patrol on the outskirts of Bejar refused to let them return to their homes. When they argued, he tried to take them captive. The officer even took a swipe at Smith with his sword, wounding him slightly on the arm. Smith retaliated by using the butt of his rifle to knock the fool out of his saddle before he and Arnold galloped away.

He joined the revolution the next day, telling Austin that

the Mexicans "acted rascally with me." Erastus "Deaf" Smith had been acting rascally with them ever since.

Pushing thoughts of the past out of his mind, Smith turned to his companion, "Boy" Kirkup, riding at his side and staring at him with hero worship in his eyes, as usual. Smith knew that one of these days he had to find a way for the youngster to recognize his own worth.

"Santa Anna leadin' those men we just left means there'll be couriers ridin' back and forth. He's a man who likes to keep firm control of everything he can reach, one of those who thinks that if he didn't have the idea then it can't be much good. I'd like to grab us one of them messengers, preferably one carryin' Santa Anna's orders to his other generals instead of goin' the other way. That should sure enough tell us what he's up to."

"How will we do that," Kirkup asked? "Won't they be extra cautious? They already know we're around somewhere."

Now that was a sensible question, thought Smith. The lad's comin' along.

"We follow, but not so close that they know we're still here," he replied. "Pretty soon, they'll either figure we left or forget about us all together. The Mexicans are all divided, with Urrea, Sesma and the others to the south and west, so any couriers will be ridin' out that way. We'll wait, be patient, and see if we can't pick one off."

20

JOINED BY HENRY KARNES, who happened to be tracking the same Mexican force and spotted their trail, they got their chance the next day.

Using his telescope, Smith saw three riders on the other side of a small bayou.

"Mexicans, and finely mounted, too," announced Smith. The three scouts had dismounted while they watched the riders from the tall weeds lining the bayou, careful to stay low so they wouldn't be seen. "Judgin' by the quality of the horses and the bulgin' saddlebags, I'd say they're deliverin' some corre … corre … what's the damn word, Boy?"

"Correspondence?" suggested Kirkup.

"That's it exactly," agreed Smith. "Henry, you spend some time with Boy here and I guarantee it'll expand your vocabulary, which it sorely needs."

"My vocabulary's already expanded enough," grumbled Karnes, who could read and write after a fashion and thought that quite sufficient for his needs. "I already know all the words I can use. Instead of wastin' time tryin' to teach me what I got no use for, why don't I take the young professor here, get up ahead of them Mexicans and cross the bayou while you get over on their backside? We'll take a couple of shots at em, send the three of 'em runnin' back toward you, and between us we can round 'em up nice as you please."

"Why don't we just shoot them out of the saddle and take the saddlebags," asked Kirkup? "Wouldn't that be easier and faster?"

Karnes and Smith looked at each other. "You tell him, Deaf."

"That's not a bad question, Boy. You're right, it's the easier way and there's many a man who'd do just that. But sometimes what a messenger knows is just as valuable as anything he's carryin'," Smith said. "In my experience, dead men don't have a lot to say."

"But won't they fight," Kirkup asked? "I mean, it's only three on three."

"Out numbered, ain't they," laughed Karnes. "Their mission is to deliver what they've been trusted with, not to get killed. They'll do everything they can to avoid a fight, and rightly so, which is why we should be able to take 'em."

"That's enough talkin'," Smith declared. With the Mexican riders out of sight, he mounted his horse and headed toward the bayou. "I'll cross here. You two go up ahead. Remember, if you have to shoot anything, shoot the horses."

Which was more or less what happened.

Karnes and Kirkup rode hard to get well ahead of the couriers before crossing the bayou and hiding in the tall grass. After a similar crossing back where they left him, Smith hid in a clump of cottonwoods, dismounted, and waited.

When the Mexican riders were 100 yards away, Karnes and Kirkup rose out of the grass and fired two shots. "Close, but not too close," as Karnes ordered. "We don't want to kill one by accident."

The couriers didn't hesitate. They yanked their mounts to

a stop, wheeled their horses, and galloped back the way they came, hoping to find an unopposed route to their destination. Karnes and Kirkup raced after them, with Kirkup's extra rifle and one pistol each in reserve.

From his position in the cottonwoods, Smith's rifle cracked and one of the Mexican horses went down, with the rider lying stunned and flat in the grass.

"Quick, Boy, take down another horse before they get out of range," yelled Karnes.

Kirkup pulled his horse to a halt, hooves skidding along the soft earth. He dropped the reins, grasped his rifle in his right hand and drew it from the soft leather scabbard, vaulting from the saddle in almost the same motion. He threw the rifle up, and, as was the style of shooting he learned back home in Yorkshire, pulled the trigger the instant that horse and rider were in his sights.

Karnes waved his hat and shouted in triumph. "More'n 300 yards if it's a foot. That's fine shootin'!"

Not knowing where the shot had come from and assuming that he must be surrounded, the third rider stopped and threw up his hands.

As they gathered the contents of the packed saddlebags into one large bag to be carried by Kirkup, Karnes noticed that one of the saddlebags was inscribed with the name WB Travis.

The red-haired scout ran his fingers across the familiar named burned deep into the leather. "Well look what we got here," he said with a hard-eyed glare at the downcast Mexicans, who assumed that they would be killed because that's what Santa Anna did to his prisoners. "These boys must have been at the Alamo. Maybe one of 'em killed Buck?"

"Let's hear what they have to say," Smith said, launching a volley of questions in Spanish at the prisoners.

After a few minutes, Smith told his companions what he learned. "The tall one is a captain, Miguel Bachiller, a *correo* from the government in Mexico City. He was supposed to get on back there but Santa Anna pressed him into service, which made him not think much of *El Presidente*. The one next to him is his own personal guard, who was just doin' what he was ordered. Even before we caught him, he wanted nothin' more than to go home. The other one claims to be one of Juan Seguin's boys. Says he was off on leave to tend to his family near Gonzales when Sesma's men captured him and forced him to be their guide by holdin' his wife and children hostage. He says Travis' saddlebag was given to Bachiller by somebody on Santa Anna's staff, already full of papers and such. None of 'em were at the Alamo."

"You believe that, Deaf," asked Karnes, who was waving his pistol like he couldn't wait to use it? "The one who says he belongs to Seguin might just be a deserter. Bastard'll say anything to save his life. They all would."

Kirkup decided that it was a good time to say nothing. Karnes was in such a rage at finding Travis' saddlebag that it seemed best to keep his mouth shut.

Smith took a long look at the third Mexican. "Yes, I do believe him, at least partly. He's one of our *Tejanos*, for sure. I've seen him around before. When we get back, Seguin will know if he's tellin' the truth."

Smith lifted a long braided rope from where it was wound around his saddle horn and passed it to Kirkup.

"Boy, cut this in sections and tie their arms behind their backs. Make sure and tie 'em at the elbows. If they try to make a break it's a lot harder to run that way. They'll find ridin' uncomfortable, but right now I don't give a damn."

The six men made what under normal circumstances was

almost a two-day ride back to the army in one day of hard travel. Smith weighed less that Karnes or Kirkup, so one Bachiller rode behind him on his mare. The two others doubled up on the extra horse captured with the couriers. Despite the extra weight, they pushed hard. The only stops were to water and feed the horses.

They rode into camp hot, thirsty, hungry and exhausted. Dismounting in the middle of camp, Smith and Karnes agreed that it was best to take the captured correspondence directly to General Houston, brushing aside questions from the curious men who quickly gathered around the scouts and their prisoners.

"Boy, you stay here and guard these three till we get back," Smith said. "I want nobody talkin' to 'em and nobody layin' a hand on 'em. Understand?"

Seeing Kirkup's nod, Karnes and Smith went in search of the general. After a few minutes, a mob of at least 50 men gathered around the prisoners and a nervous Kirkup, who several times warned the growing crowd that it was Smith's orders that they keep their distance.

Invoking the scout's name only worked for so long. As the men edged closer in a night lit by campfires and torches, Jedidiah Tilton, a swarthy black-bearded Kentuckian dressed in greasy buckskins, noticed the saddlebag with the name WB Travis burned into the leather. Before Kirkup could stop him, Tilton pulled the saddlebag off the horse and waved it high in one hand so the rest of the men could see it.

"Look at this, boys! Seems like these Mexican sons-a-bitches were at the Alamo. It's Buck Travis' own saddlebag. What do you think we should do about it?"

With Tilton, who had a reputation as a hard and dangerous man, leading the way, the mob surged forward, with cries of "Hang 'em" ringing in the night. Tilton had somehow acquired a rope that he was waving in the air along with the Travis saddlebag.

As the mob pressed closer, forcing Kirkup back while the prisoners cowered behind him, in a deep raspy voice Tilton bellowed, "Get out of the way, you snot nosed English shit! We mean to hang these greasers right now!"

Pressed to close to raise his rifle, Kirkup drew his pistol from his belt and pointed it at Tilton's bearded face, so that the barrel pressed hard into the big man's eye, which stopped him in his tracks.

With a determined authority that he didn't know he possessed, Kirkup cocked the pistol and declared, "If any of you take one more step, I'll blow Tilton's ugly face off."

No one moved or said a word. The silence was eerie after the noisy bloodlust of a moment before. The scene seemed frozen in time with neither side willing to give way until Smith, Karnes and a have dozen men bustled up to take the prisoners to the general.

As the muttering mob broke up and drifted into the night, and Tilton backed away with an angry glare as he rubbed his sore eye, the delighted Smith slapped Kirkup on the back so hard that it almost knocked him over.

"Granville, if anyone ever calls you 'Boy' again, they'll damn well answer to me."

21

"GENERAL, if what I've read so far holds up then this is as good as gold," declared Lorenzo de Zavala Jr.

The vice president' son was a recent addition to Houston's staff, giving some relief to the badly over-worked Hockley. Well educated, fluent in English and Spanish, and experienced beyond his years from working with his father, a Mexican politician and diplomat before he joined the rebellion, the young de Zavala was the ideal candidate to translate all the letters, messages and documents intercepted by Smith, Karnes and Kirkup.

Shuffling through the papers, a broad smile spread across de Zavalas' beardless face.

"I will need two or three hours to go through every scrap, but it looks like this tells us everything we could possibly want, including Santa Anna's troop dispositions, his orders to his subordinates, what he plans to do, and how he plans to do it. Having this information in our possession is practically the same as reading his mind. There also are many letters home from Santa Anna's officers – husbands to wives and lovers to mistresses – all of them show how desperate they are to bring an end to the rebellion."

Houston, De Zavala, Hockley, Rusk, Smith, Karnes, Seguin and Sherman were gathered outside Houston's tent, with one lamp set in the middle to light the rough circle. Sherman, de Zavala, and Rusk sat on camp stools, the rest on the ground, with one exception. Houston preferred to stand, which made it easier to dominate the meeting as he paced back and forth. He had guards posted on the perimeter to insure privacy while they assessed exactly what they had in this paper bonanza. He'd meet with the other senior officers later, as soon as he was certain about the contents and what to do about it.

"I don't see what good this does us," Rusk said, mumbling as he used the lantern to light a cigar. "Once Santa Anna knows that we're captured his couriers, won't he just change his plans?"

"It'll be a while before he knows," replied Houston. "When the couriers don't show, the other generals will likely wait a day or two to make sure they're not just late for some reason. Then they'll send riders to Santa Anna to find out what happened. If we're lucky, the whole thing'll take a several days of goin' back and forth. Even if he does change his plans, which he might anyway, this should tell us who's where with what and how many."

Karnes and Smith talked quietly between themselves, with Karnes making sure that his face was in the lantern's light so Smith could understand him. Like Kirkup, Karnes had figured out that Smith was a lip reader. He didn't necessarily have to hear everything to understand, or at least get the gist, although it was always best to be sure. When they finished their brief conversation, Karnes spoke for them both.

"General, Deaf and me think they may never know, at least not so it matters," he said. "Deaf says the Mexican couriers don't run on a particular schedule or we'd have taken more of 'em than we have before now. That's been my experience, too. It seems likely that it'll be a long while before Santa Anna's generals miss what they didn't know was comin' in the first place."

As he considered the possibilities, Houston used his clasp knife to slice a hunk of chewing tobacco off a twist he carried in his pocket, but thought better of it and put it back. He never really liked chewing tobacco. It was just something to do in the absence of alcohol, which he dearly missed. The little pleasure he got from it wasn't worth the trouble. Maybe this was a good time to give it up?

"Tom, you got another one of those cigars?" Houston asked.

Rusk nodded and handed one over. Like Rusk, Houston used the lantern to light up. It gave him time to think, too.

"Lorenzo, you say you need at least two hours, maybe three, to get through everything in that pile?"

When de Zavala nodded, the general's response was brusque.

"You've got one hour." He waved his arm to take in the material gathered at de Zavala's feet. "If this information is as valuable as we think it is, and from what I've seen already I believe that to be the case, upon Lorenzo's confirmation this army will be on the march very soon."

"Hockley, tell the other senior officers there will be a conference in one hour." He motioned toward de Zavala. "Lorenzo, you will give us your conclusions at that time. And don't tell me what you think I want to hear; whatever you find, say it straight out. If it holds up, this could be our chance and we'll have to make the most of it. We may never get another one as good. But we don't want to walk into anything half-cocked either."

As the meeting broke up, Houston added two more thoughts.

"I want no word of this to the men, not yet," he said. "Santa Anna has his spies just as we have ours. I don't want him to know what we have in our possession. Nothing said here is to be revealed to anyone else until I say so. Is that understood? And before we march, I want to get rid of all excess baggage that might slow us down, including" – Houston waved toward his tent – "that."

When Sherman rose to leave with the others, Houston motioned for him to stay behind. As always, he wondered how the man managed to stay so dapper. By now, most of the men were dressed in rags, even the officers. Houston himself was down to two coats; the buckskin and a black cloth dress coat that was practically worn through. He usually wore moccasins even in the rain because the soles of his boots were starting to go and he wanted to save them.

"Colonel, what's the condition of our cavalry," Houston asked? "If this develops into something significant I will need your people more than ever."

To Houston's amusement, Sherman puffed himself up like a pigeon.

"General, we are ready for anything you want of us," he announced. "I have absolute confidence in my men, even that new one you sent me, Lamar."

"And how is Maribeau Bounaparte Lamar workin' out?" Houston lingered on each syllable of Lamar's name, as if mocking it and taking pleasure in it at the same time.

"That sorry son of a bitch practically just got here and he already wants my job," complained Sherman, showing more bitterness than he probably intended.

Good, thought Houston. That's just what I had in mind. With Sherman busy fighting off an ambitious rival like Lamar he won't have time to put me in his sights. He might even do what he's told for a while.

"I've no doubt of that, Colonel," agreed Houston, feigning sympathy. "I suspect that he wants mine, too."

When Sherman left, Houston had another thought and called for Hockley.

"Have you started spreadin' the word about the officers meeting?"

"No, sir, not yet," Hockley replied, wondering if his unpredictable general was about to scold him for being slow to carry out his order. "I was just about to."

"Don't bother," Houston said, waving him off. "I've decided against it."

He saw Hockley's quizzical look, but ignored it. He just didn't want to hear all the windbag effusions at another meeting where everyone criticized this, that, or the other thing, but at the same time did everything they could to avoid taking responsibility or committing themselves to anything that might be controversial later. It was as if some of the officers were trying to predict the future and avoid the present at the same time. In Houston's long-held opinion, most meetings weren't necessary; they didn't enhance progress, they slowed it down or stopped it altogether. Virtually all of his officers claimed to be eager to fight, and he knew that many of them really were. But when the time came he suspected that at least half of them would find some excuse why the army would do better to avoid a fight, the risk being more than they could bear. Besides, Houston saw what he had to do clear enough. There was no reason to ask for opinions and he never liked having to explain himself.

While de Zavala muttered outside as he went over the captured documents, struggling to find the right blend of attention to detail and enough speed to finish in only an hour, inside the tent Houston spread out a map to consider his options.

Santa Anna's overall intentions were obvious from the beginning, or at least once the Alamo fell and the doomed Fannin was slaughtered with his men. Basically it was a three-pronged strategy designed to overwhelm what remained of the Texian forces. Urrea moved north more or less along the coast with about 1,400 men while Gaona's 700 to 800 men swept down from the north, and 1,200 men commanded by Santa Anna and Sesma pushed through the center of Texas. There were other Mexican forces scattered about, all the way down to the Rio Grande, in fact. But, except for Cos, who had at least 650 men within a two-day march, just now they were too far apart to be useful to each other.

As Houston assessed the map, it was clear that Santa Anna should have waited at the Brazos River, probably at Fort Bend, to concentrate his forces, which then truly would have been overwhelming. But when *El Presidente* learned of the Texas government's flight to Harrisburg he impatiently set out ahead with about 500 infantry, 100 cavalry and one brass 12-pound cannon that the Mexicans called *el estandar de oro*, or the Gold Standard, to try to capture Burnet and the cabinet. Once he got out front, he stayed there. As a result, for the time being Santa Anna's great superiority in numbers did not exist. In his arrogance, he had isolated himself with a small force, although he did seem to be aware of his mistake. According to Smith and Karnes, the Mexican general ordered Cos to join him at Lynch's Ferry on Buffalo Bayou.

Houston was pleased to see that a bit of misdirection he gambled on had worked. He'd ordered that the word be quietly spread that he intended to defend Lynch's Ferry, which he claimed to be the key to the eastern settlements in Texas. The ferry really wasn't vital to anything, but Houston wanted Santa Anna to turn his army that way in his effort to run down the Texians.

What made it tricky was that the false information had to be put out in a way so that it was not widely known, which would help convince Santa Anna that he'd discovered a secret. That was why Houston put the subtle Seguin in charge. The clever *Tejano* leader pretended to accidentally let the word slip out to three newspaper printers in Harrisburg who were trying to put out the last edition of The Telegraph and Texas Register before they ran like everyone else. It was well known that such people can't keep a secret. If they weren't blabber-mouths, they wouldn't be in the newspaper business in the first place.

When Seguin lied again and assured them that no Mexicans were nearby and they had plenty of time to print their newspaper, the trio lingered too long, which was just what Seguin wanted. When Santa Anna suddenly appeared in Harrisburg and took the printers prisoner, after a minimum of "persuasion" they told him two things. The first was that Burnet and the cabinet were safe aboard the steamer Cayuga, heading down Buffalo Bayou to the San Jacinto River and then probably on to Galveston Bay. The second was that Houston intended to defend Lynch's Ferry, which crossed the San Jacinto about 15 miles east of Harrisburg, in an effort to block Santa Anna's advance into east Texas.

According to what de Zavala saw in his preliminary look at the captured documents, Santa Anna intended to move on to New Washington, for some reason thinking that Burnet might have gone back be there, then double back to Lynch's Ferry, where he could destroy the Texian army and end the rebellion once and for all.

Houston didn't give a damn about defending the ferry. But the printers didn't know that and now neither did Santa

Anna, who was already moving in that direction by way of New Washington. Once he destroyed New Washington – which he almost certainly would, that being Santa Anna's way – he'd march to Lynch's Ferry, where he'd link with Cos. If he didn't find Houston and his army then he'd likely march on to Galveston and take it, hopefully before Houston discovered his intentions, leaving Texas without a port. At the same time, it was clear that Seguin's hard-riding men were so effective at screening the Texian movements that Santa Anna had no firm idea of where Houston actually was. All he had was the false report of Houston's intentions.

A intercepted letter to General Filisola from Santa Anna showed how wrong *El Presidente* was about what Houston was dong: *"Due to reports which I have gathered at this point, I have no doubts that the entitled General Houston who was at Groce's Crossing with a force of five to six hundred men, has moved toward Nacogdoches and should have left yesterday in that direction. However, since he is escorting families and supplies in ox-drawn wagons, his march is slow. The Trinity River, moreover, should detain him many days."*

These games within games were all ridiculously complicated and even enjoyable, assuming they worked. If the Texians moved quickly, they might be able to bring Santa Anna into battle before he was reinforced by Cos. Houston still didn't like risking everything on one battle. His critics were right about that. If they lost the revolution was all but over. But the opportunity was too good to pass up.

Houston's belief that the moment was close at hand was reinforced by Seguin's long conversation with the three prisoners, who loosened up considerably when they realized that they wouldn't be killed after all, especially once they saw Kirkup's bravery in keeping the lynch mob at bay.

He made a mental note to see that young man promoted.

Kirkup kept calm and stood his ground when many other men would have panicked or given in. Behavior such as that should be rewarded, although it was unfortunate that it took an Englishman to do it, which illustrated a larger problem that had nagged at Houston for some time. It was disappointing how most of the men in the army came from somewhere other than Texas. They had recruits from all over the United States, although mostly from the South. There also were Germans, one or two Englishmen, a few Italians, and many *Tejanos*, mostly serving under Seguin, whose support and intimate knowledge of the country was invaluable. They had Poles, Austrians, and freed slaves. They had men from practically everywhere, it seemed, but not as many Texians as he'd hoped.

True, many of the men of fighting age were with their families in this perilous time and Houston understood. But that didn't explain it all. It was as if too many of these people somehow expected to win their independence from Mexico without having to fight for it. But didn't independence require sacrifice? Of course, it always did and always would. There also were too many Texians like that pig Donoho, people who had grown so fat and prosperous that they didn't want change. Why would they? There was no profit in.

Along that same line, it turned out that one of the prisoners *had* served with Seguin, although he had no family to protect, as he claimed. The man was granted extended leave several weeks ago only because Seguin didn't trust him and none of his comrades wanted him around. There was little doubt that he'd changed sides and volunteered as a guide to serve with Santa Anna. Houston turned him over to the *Tejanos* do as they pleased. It would not be pleasant.

According to the three prisoners, Santa Anna's army was in poor shape. Supplies were scarce and there was no medicine or care for the sick and wounded. Being so far from Mexico, the Mexicans had to live off the land and there wasn't much left after the Texian army passed. Even with so many settlers engaged in the humiliating Runaway Scrape, as it was known, what scraps they left behind certainly wasn't enough to feed an invading army.

As hard as it was at the time, it looked like burning Gonzales and San Felipe was the right thing to do after all. The Mexicans were worn out from all the marching in bad weather as they chased Houston's army. The fights at the Alamo and against Fannin took a heavy toll, too. Apparently Santa Anna still had hopes that he could capture Burnet and the cabinet and end the rebellion in one stroke. Houston wanted him to keep trying. Chasing the elusive president at the same time they chased the Texian army would only wear down the Mexicans even more than they already were. Houston knew that this army – his army – was all that mattered. As long as it was in the field the revolution lived. He did not tell anyone because no one would understand, but he would not be disappointed if Burnet *was* captured. It would serve old *Wetumpka* right and do no real damage at all.

Bachiller, the courier from Mexico City, turned out to be well connected. He told Seguin that Santa Anna was feeling political pressure from the capital, which probably was one reason for his reckless haste. *El Presidente* had too many rivals at home for him to stay away for too long. A man who rises by treachery always fears it himself. There was no one the dictator trusted to run the country in his absence and he was too far away for effective communication. He was eager to end the rebellion and get back to Mexico City before his rivals turned on him and that eagerness made him take chances.

So Houston's army was getting stronger while Santa Anna was growing weaker. In his zeal and vanity the self-styled

Napoleon of the West had run too far out in front. Yes, he could be reinforced, but would it happen soon enough? Even Napoleon was beaten in his day.

Santa had lost the initiative and he didn't even know it.

The time was coming. Houston could feel it.

22

Houston's thoughts were interrupted by Sherman's voice from outside the tent.

"General, may I come in?"

Houston sighed. Another futile session with Sherman was not a pleasant prospect. Every one of their conversations was exactly the same. All they did was cover the same tired old ground. It was like trying to plant in a field where nothing would gro.

Like most wealthy men, the fine-featured Sherman wore a sense of entitlement like fine new clothes. He thought that because he paid for the men he raised out of his own pocket it made him a military expert.

But it was Houston's policy to be available to almost anyone at almost any time and there was nothing he could do about it.

"Of course."

Sherman entered the tent and sat on the cot at Houston's waved invitation.

"You canceled the officer's meeting," Sherman said, his sharp tone turning the statement into an accusation.

When Houston didn't reply, the Kentuckian kept talking. "General, I think you're just settin' us up to run away again and you don't have the gumption to face the officers and explain yourself. You always claim that you're ready to fight and it'll happen any day now, but then you refuse to do it and all we do is run some more. By my calculation, we've already covered more than seven hundred miles, almost all of it goin' the wrong way. If it was up to you, most of us think you'd let Santa Anna run us clear out of Texas."

Once again, Houston said nothing, knowing that his silence would wind Sherman even tighter than he already was; in his agitation, the man was practically bouncing on the cot. Houston wasn't sure that the frail wood frame could stand it much longer.

"General, I've come to tell you that the men and officers just won't take it anymore. Sure, there's a few who'll stay with you, men like Tom Rusk and your boy Hockley. He follows you around like a dog. Young de Zavala, too, I expect. But most of the rest of the senior officers – includin' me, Jess Billingsley, Ed Burleson, John Forbes, Mosley Baker, and Wiley Martin - have had enough runnin'. If you don't stand and fight soon, you'll lose your army. History will damn you to hell, and, by God, you'll deserve it."

If Sherman expected anger, he didn't get it and received a full blast of scorn instead. Houston leaned forward, put his elbows on his knees, and stared hard into the colonel's eyes.

"Colonel Sherman, I'm happy to hear that you now speak for every man in this army. The responsibility must be burdensome for a modest soul like yourself. And by the way, now that we're on the subject, would you remind me of the vast experience that makes you such a military expert? It seems to have slipped my mind. Exactly how many battles have you been in? Have you ever even *seen* a hostile army?

Have you ever been wounded? Or shot at? We both know that the answer to all those questions is no, don't we?"

"Sherman, I command this army, no one else. I have the responsibility and the authority and I will not give it up or explain myself, not to you and not to anyone. We will fight at the right time and right place and it will be my decision as to when and where that will be. And I don't give a damn if you like it or not."

Suddenly feeling so weary that his whole body ached, Houston sat up straight and rubbed his eyes with his index finger and thumb.

"You like to babble about history, and how you're so confident that history will say this and history will say that. Do you know who writes history? The winners. You don't like me and I don't like you. You think I'm a coward and I think you're a blowhard. So be it. The men bellyache and the officers grumble and I don't care because none of it matters. That's what armies have done since the time of Caesar. If we win, you and I and all the rest of us will be heroes. We'll be the founding fathers of a new nation and there'll be plenty of glory for all of us, even you. If we lose, I will get the blame. No one will say that Sydney Sherman was at fault, will they? It will be Sam Houston who failed. I will be infamous, and not for the first time either. But it won't matter because Texas will be lost and more than likely we'll all be dead and history can say what it pleases."

The two men glared at each other for a moment before Sherman's gaze dropped and he rose from the cot shaking his head.

"Houston, all I have to say is that you'd better know what you're doin'."

"If I don't, we'll find out soon enough, won't we?" Houston replied. "There is one last thing. George Washington Hockley is no man's dog. He is a high-ranking officer in this army and in the future you will speak of him with the respect he deserves. "

"And now, Colonel Sherman, you ... are ... dismissed."

23

HE VOLUNTEERED FOR IT, but Henry Karnes didn't think this new assignment would come to much. He just needed to stay active. There were times when it felt like his body couldn't contain all of his energy. Even when he was in repose, his foot bounced up and down or his fingers drummed on the nearest hard surface.

Like everyone, Karnes knew about the argument between Sherman and Houston. Voices were raised and too many people heard to keep it a secret. When Sherman was ordered by the general to take 100 mounted volunteers and cross over Comanche Bayou to make sure there was no Mexican force in the area, Karnes assumed it was the general's way of keeping Sherman out of the way for a time, though, if passable, it might be a quicker route for their march too.

According to the orders, if unopposed they could push on to Vince's Bayou, where a handful of Mexican cavalry had been spotted by Seguin's men two days ago. Depending on what they found, they might even press on to Lynchburg, if that was possible.

Although Karnes was certain that any Mexican riders that

wandered this close were long gone and hadn't seen anything important, and the assignment was Houston's way of keeping the cavalry active and get Sherman out of his sight for a while – even before the argument, the bad blood between them was well known - he understood the need to be sure and volunteered to lead an advance party of 20 men.

Although they should have expected it, crossing Comanche Bayou was much more difficult than anyone thought. Swollen by the recent rain, the bayou's water was so high that it spooked most of the horses when they couldn't find bottom for long stretches. The rising water had destroyed most of the snake nests in the area and poisonous reptiles were swimming everywhere. One man was bitten and two others came close to it. Even the good swimmers among the horses got panicky after a while and all the snakes didn't do the men much good either. After struggling all day long with one false start after another, Karnes' exhausted men finally made it after sending all their powder across on a hastily built raft so that it wouldn't get soaked during the wild crossing that left all of them soaking wet and covered with oozy black crud.

Before Sherman's men could follow the next morning, Karnes had his men fire three shots in the air five seconds apart, a pre-arranged signal indicating that the route was all-but impassable and that they should stay put, heading back for camp when Karnes' men re-joined them. The problem was that on the way to Lynchburg, Karnes knew that they would have to cross Sims Bayou, too, which promised to be even more difficult. With all the rain in the last few weeks, it was almost impossible to say where one bayou stopped and the other started. Even if there were a few Mexican riders around, and Karnes didn't think there was, they'd only be stuck in the bog, too.

Getting back across would be impossible in the dark, so

Karnes' men settled down to spend a lonely night on the other side of the bayou, isolated from the rest of the force.

Private Joseph Armaugh was assigned the first advance guard detail. An 18-year-old who left from Limerick, Ireland, at age 12, Armaugh settled in Ohio with his family. He was working as an apprentice for a tanner in Louisville, Kentucky, when Stephen Austin passed through, raising men, arms, and money for the rebellion.

Armaugh didn't know what he wanted out of life, but he'd quickly learned that it didn't include the tanning trade, which mostly consisted of stinking hard work from dawn to dusk. With a letter of introduction from Austin, he joined the Texian army at Groce's Plantation, where he was assigned to the company commanded by Captain William Patton. When Sherman asked for 100 volunteers to go on a special assignment, Armaugh was one of the first to step up, and he was thrilled to wind up riding with the legendary Henry Karnes.

His sergeant, Aaron Blair, who was only a year or two older than Armaugh much vastly more experienced, escorted him out to his station in the deep woods a half-mile in advance of the company.

"We don't know how many Mexicans might be out here, or if any of 'em are out here," Blair explained. "For all we know, there aren't any Mexicans within 25 miles. On the other hand, there might be a hundred of 'em hidin' in the trees and waitin' to pounce on your pale Irish butt. You just stay alert until you're relieved and give the alarm if you see anything. Fire a shot, hug the ground, and try not to get killed. It won't take us long to come up."

After spending an hour alone in blackest night he'd ever seen, a half mile out in front of his comrades, Armaugh was so jumpy that he felt like he might leap out of his own skin. He knew, he just knew, that he was surrounded by the enemy. Not being able to see his hand in front of his face in the darkness only made it worse. Certain that he would be murdered any minute, he managed to convince himself that some stealthy Mexican was sneaking up behind so that he could slit his throat, leaving poor Joseph Armaugh alone and bleeding to death out in the middle of nowhere, killed almost before his life had a chance to get started. He spent most of the time on watch turning this way and that way and back again in fear, like a child's spinning top. Why in God's name did he ever leave Louisville? Being a tanner was a nice respectable trade. It was safe, too, nobody ever tried to kill a tanner.

Armaugh practically rocketed out of his badly tattered boots when he heard something rustle in the woods ahead. It was something big, too. A horse, or maybe horses.

And this time, it wasn't his imagination. Armaugh was sure of it. The noise was too real, it was coming his way, and it was already too close. Mouth dry and hands sweating, he lifted his rifle, aimed it at the darkness in the general direction of the sound, and pulled back the hammer with a satisfying click.

"Give the password or I fire," he shouted, immediately feeling like a 10 kinds of fool when he remembered that there was no password. It was just something that he thought a guard should say and came out of his mouth before he could stop it.

Whoever it was showed no fear at all as they boldly came even closer and the sound grew louder, with branches pushed aside and twigs crackling on the ground.

Jesus, Mary and Joseph! There must be at least a dozen of them out there! In Armaugh's excitement, his trembling finger prematurely pulled the trigger and the rifle erupted in a mighty roar that stunned his senses. The unexpected kick almost knocked him on his backside. It was the first time he shot his weapon since he joined the army.

Faster than Armaugh thought possible, Karnes and four other men galloped to his side.

Throwing himself off his horse with his rifle in one hand to kneel at Armaugh's side, Karnes whispered, "What'd you see?"

"Sounded like a lot of 'em out there, sir. I don't know. Maybe a dozen or more. I took a shot but don't know if I hit anything."

"I'll go have a look," Karnes said, staring intently into the darkness. "The rest of you boys stay here. Don't get all jittery and shoot me when I come back."

Without a sound, the scout glided into the night, the most dangerous looking character Armaugh had ever seen. One man against a dozen and he didn't seem to care.

Karnes returned a few minutes later, his rifle casually leaning on his shoulder and a big grin on his face.

"What'd you see, sir," asked Armaugh, who was so anxious that he didn't noticed Karnes' casual attitude?

"It was a good enough shot, right through the brain," Karnes replied. "Or it would have been if you'd been able to see what you were shootin' at. Come tomorrow, it'll be good eatin', too."

Laughing at Armaugh's stupefied look, Karnes explained, "You shot yourself a cow."

For the rest of the campaign, Joseph Armaugh was known as "Moo."

24

THEY LEFT BEHIND 248 men who were injured or too ill to march, along with any equipment that might slow them down, including the second tent that Houston gave up during the campaign. He wanted to pick the ground where they would meet Santa Anna and they had to move fast and get ahead of him to do it. Looking at the map, it almost certainly would be somewhere near Lynchburg.

But there was another issue Houston had to deal with, and it was not an easy one to resolve. Ever since Wylie Martin's men rejoined the army after their failed defense of the river ford, Martin loudly and repeatedly proclaimed that he could no longer serve under such a "gutless" commander who was "afraid to fight," although he didn't do anything about it except talk.

It was even worse after the discovery of Travis' saddlebag, which seemed to almost unhinge the man. Almost everyone who knew Buck Travis took it hard, of course. There was something so sad and lonely about it. Finding this one small possession was somehow more poignant than finding nothing at all. But Houston was puzzled about why it seemed to affect

Martin more than anyone until he remembered that Martin and Travis were good friends. Given the difference in the ages – 20 years at least - it was more like a father-son relationship. Martin, who fancied himself an artist of sorts, had even drawn a likeness of Travis a year or so ago that he still carried with him like it was some kind of holy artifact. If you squinted, held it just so in the light, and didn't demand too much fealty to accuracy or detail, it was not a bad resemblance.

Under normal circumstances, Houston wouldn't give a damn about Martin's feelings or opinions, much less his friendship with Travis, who he regarded as just this side of a dangerous lunatic, a vainglorious boy who got himself, and a lot of other good men, killed for no good reason. But Martin's unending vitriol might undo all the good that had been accomplished in forging the army into a diamond-hard fighting unit instead of an undisciplined rabble where each man thought he was his own general and acted like it.

At least Sherman had the sense to keep his carping mostly confined to his similar thinking cronies in complaint. Martin was like a fire-and-brimstone preacher who spread his gospel wherever two or more were gathered together, no matter if they wanted to be converted.

It was Rusk, with Hockley's help, who had the idea.

As was his habit just before sundown on most days, Houston was walking the camp, accompanied by Rusk and Hockley, who was furiously tugging on his dark beard, a habit whenever he was nervous or working out a difficult problem. Given that Hockley was almost always in a state of turmoil about something, Houston marveled that he hadn't snatched himself bald faced.

Suddenly, without warning or preamble, Rusk pushed Houston to "do something about that man Martin and his big mouth. It better be soon, too, before he sours the whole army."

Before he could restrain himself, Houston took out on Rusk some of the frustration that he felt toward Martin, Sherman, and the rest of the malcontents.

"That's a splendid idea, Tom," Houston snapped. "I never would have thought of it myself. Now tell me how to go about it. It doesn't take much of a man to complain without offering a solution, does it? We all know what we *should* do. The problem is figuring out *how* to do it. If you've got something to say that might do some good, spit it out. If not, then stop telling me what I already know."

The hot flash of Houston's anger usually was enough to cow most men into silence. He didn't expect a reply, especially the one he got.

"Sir, Hockley and I might have a solution," Rusk said, nodding toward Hockley, who was walking on Houston's other side.

Rusk was remarkably calm considering that his general did everything but bite his head off. But then Tom Rusk was always a hard man to rattle. It was one of the things that Houston appreciated most about him.

"As you know all too well, we have hundreds of refugees following the army, with more coming every day. They're with us and not with us at the same time. Mostly they stick around because they don't know where else to go. They're a drain on our resources and everybody knows it. They slow us down, they eat our food, and almost every night a few of our men go prowling among them looking for women. It's probably our biggest discipline problem."

"Yes, I know all that, gentlemen," Houston said, still feeling his pique from a moment ago. "Kindly get to the point."

"Well, sir, we thought you might consider puttin' Martin in charge of the refugees," Hockley suggested. "It was more Tom's idea than mine. I mean, it was all Tom's idea, but I think it's a good one. Whatever our opinion of him, the man is energetic and good at organization. So let him be the shepherd who herds those people away from us, somewhere to a safer place, maybe close to the border so they can easily get across into Louisiana, if it comes to that. He'd be doing a valuable service and we'd be rid of him and the refugees at the same time."

Houston stopped in his tracks, glancing around to make sure that they weren't overheard. The general's daily walks through camp just before sundown were so routine that no one seemed to be paying attention as the men lit their fires and began to think about supper. The day's march through the mire and mud was so difficult that most of the men were too exhausted to care.

As Houston turned it over in his mind, the idea was almost too good. Its sheer perfection made him suspicious.

"So the two of you worked it all out all on your own, did you?"

Houston wasn't sure if he should be pleased or disapproving at the way they teamed up on him. Remembering his recent speech to Hockley about taking the initiative, he realized that he'd been hoist on his own petard, whatever the hell a petard was. It was a phrase he'd heard somewhere and liked.

"Tell me, gentlemen, is it your belief that would Martin do it? The solution is almost too perfect. Do you think he'd deliberately choose to miss his chance to play a part in the battle that will decide everything?"

Rusk and Hockley looked at each other in obvious agreement.

"Martin despises you, general, and everybody knows it," Rusk explained. "He's not like some of the others who want you out of the way mostly so they can advance. He truly doesn't believe that you will ever fight Santa Anna. In his mind, there is no chance for him to miss. He probably would have left us already but he doesn't want to seem to be running away after so long criticizing you for doing just that. An order from you to take charge of the refugees would give him an excuse to leave us."

Houston winced at Rusk's candor. He never thought of himself as someone to be despised. Some men didn't mind it. Andrew Jackson knew that he was despised by many, took a kind of fierce pride in it, and returned the favor with interest. Houston was never able to shrug it off, although he sometimes pretended that he did.

But Rusk was right, just the same. Whenever they came together, Martin's loathing was like a physical force. Houston's patience with the man wouldn't last much longer either. There was no doubt that the army would be better off without him. Escorting the refugees to safety, he wouldn't need to take many men with him, perhaps 50 at most. And they wouldn't need to be very good men either, a good opportunity to cull out some of the weaker characters.

Taking the general's silence as permission to continue, Hockley added, "Tom's right, sir. Give Martin an opportunity like this and he'll grab it like a free beer."

"And we really do have to do something about all these people, General," Rusk said. "As I said, this solves both problems and gives Martin a way out."

Houston laughed. He was suddenly feeling almost lighthearted with pleasure.

"I wish you hadn't put it that way, Tom," he said. "By God, I could use a beer. All right, Hockley, draw up the order and I'll sign it. Make it clear that Martin can either obey this order or go straight to hell. Either way, I want him out of camp. You can stop yanking at your beard now, too.

25

MOUNTED on Saracen at the side of the road while he munched on an apple, as he watched the men march by Houston reflected that sometimes there really was such a thing as a crossroads in life.

And this army of his was coming to one.

According to Deaf Smith, Santa Anna believed that Houston was headed for the Trinity River by way of Lynchburg on Buffalo Bayou, a reasonable assumption under the circumstances. But *El Presidente* was worried that from there Houston and his Texians would join President Burnet and the rest of the government on Galveston Island, thus escaping the mainland to safety before the Mexicans could intercept and defeat them.

To prevent it, Santa Anna intended to make the river crossing at Lynchburg before Houston got there. He also ordered a squadron of dragoons to ride ahead with orders to look out for the ragged band of "land thieves."

Houston wanted to get there first, too, but not stay ahead of Santa Anna and run away. He intended to pick the most favorable ground for the battle that would decide everything.

As a result, he whipped his men 55 miles in two days through some of the worst weather any of them had ever seen. It was an energy draining world of rain, mud and bog; although the sky did finally clear as they approached the crossroads just ahead, where the choice to be made was clear and the men knew it. On the left, the north road led away from the Mexican army, on to Nacogdoches and beyond that to the United States. If they turned right, they were marching to meet Santa Anna.

Weary as they were, a buzz passed through the ranks as the men struggled step by squishy step through the ooze that sucked at their feet, sometimes even pulling shoes away from the wearer, at least from those men who had shoes.

Which way would they go? If Houston ordered them to take the left road, would the officers obey? It was generally thought that most of the men would follow his orders, whatever they were, but that many of the officers might not. The question was how many. And what would happen then? What would Houston do if his army split in two, with some of the men going one way and some going the other? Looking at it realistically, what *could* he do about it?

A few loudmouths bragged that they knew Houston's plans. When they could not say how they knew, they found believers were in short supply. Others took guesses, while most had no idea, even those who thought that they did.

As usual, Houston kept his own counsel and told no one of his exact plans. Although Hockley, Rusk, and a few others thought they had a good sense of his intentions, following the general's unspoken command, they said nothing. It was a perfect opportunity for wagering, but no one had any money.

The road forked at the entrance to the farm of old Abraham Roberts, a widower who settled the fertile country of east Texas nine years ago. Like most settlers, he readily took the oath to become a Mexican citizen. And, like most of the settlers, he didn't give a damn about it, not much caring for government of any kind. The split was marked by a dying old tree with gnarled and mostly leafless limbs that seemed to point out both alternatives like the bony fingers of a skeleton – one way to retreat, the other to battle on a road that passed by Harrisburg on the way to Lynchburg, a little fly speck of a town that few of the men knew but that had suddenly become terribly important to them all.

It was approaching mid-day and the long line of men rumbled with rumor and opinion, everything from heated argument to knowing glances, at least from those who had the energy to spare. Tension was high and they all felt it. Which way would they go? And what would happen when they did? If they were only going to retreat again, why did Houston push them so hard? But after retreating almost 750 miles so far, what made anyone think that Old Sam would suddenly stop running here?

Houston let most of the army pass before he tossed away the apple core, gave a tug Saracen's reins, and galloped to the front of the line, the white stallion's hooves throwing big globs of mud in its wake. As he approached the front of the long snake of marching men, he saw Abraham Roberts standing at his gate at the side of the road, watching the army approach.

Someone in the front of the ranks cried, "Which road to Harrisburg, old man?"

Roberts laughed, revealing a general lack of teeth, raised his leathery hand, and pointed. "That right-hand road will carry you to Harrisburg just as straight as a compass."

With Saracen pawing at the ground as if to show that he was as eager as any of them, Houston calmly ordered, "Column right," but only a few heard him in the wild roar from the soggy mud-splattered men who, in response to Roberts' directions, cheered and took up the cry, "To the right, boys! To the right!" They were going to meet Santa Anna no matter what. The time had finally come. The running had stopped.

Fortunately, their general agreed, although many of the officers and men didn't know it.

————

ONLY THREE MILES down the road from what already was being called "the Which-way Tree," Houston spotted a large gap in the line and rode back to find the reason for the delay.

He was greeted by one of the most unusual sights of his life. A woman, whose name, he later learned, was Pamela Mann, a creature well-known in these parts, had cowed the entire crew of men who were hauling the Twin Sisters, the army's Cincinnati-made cannon, as she practically turned the air blue with her language.

"Goddam your no-account souls, you will give me my oxen this minute or I will cut your useless balls off and feed 'em to my dogs," she bellowed, waving a Bowie knife in one fist with the flair of an expert, a very angry expert. The formidable vision was mounted on a brown gelding, with a pair of holstered pistols attached to her saddle, along with a well-used shotgun in a worn leather scabbard.

Houston couldn't blame the men for not knowing how to respond, or even wanting to. She was at least six feet tall and weighed 250 pounds if she weighed an ounce. To say that she was ugly was a profound insult to ugly people everywhere. Her deeply lined face had the consistency of a potato and her powerful body resembled a badly-packed sand bag, which the faded calico dress she wore over a pair of ancientriding boots somewhat resembled.

Still astride Saracen, Houston edged to her side, tipped his hat, and inquired, "What seems to be the trouble, Ma'am?"

Turning in Houston's direction, her Bowie knife at the ready, she snarled a question of her own: "Who the hell are you?"

"Just a citizen and soldier engaged in his duty," he replied. "I take it that you believe these oxen belong to you."

"Your god-double-damned right they do," she said, waving her knife again as if she intended to carve the air to shreds. "And there ain't no *believe* about it. A couple of days ago, some big Dutchman asked me if I'd loan my team to haul these here cannon to Nacogdoches. But once I saw you boys hit that fork back a ways I knew that bastard told me a damn lie 'cause you all are headed the other direction. That won't do. No, sir, it won't. You all gonna get killed somewheres and if I don't take my team now I'll never see 'em again. I want 'em back and I want 'em back now!"

"But, ma'am, I'm afraid we can't spare them," Houston explained. "It'd be too difficult to haul the cannon otherwise. I do apologize for the man's prevarication. You will, of course, be compensated for the use of your team and I promise they will be returned to you in the best of shape."

Houston, of course, was lying, too. He couldn't promise any such thing and knew it.

And the target of his false promises was having none of it.

"I don't give a hoot in hell what you apologize for, whatever it was, prevarifuckall, and I care less than that about your damn cannon. That son-of-a-bitch lied to me. I'm takin' my team back and ain't nobody gonna stop me."

With that, she slid off her horse in the way of a mud slide, revealing pale thighs only a little smaller than a water barrel, a sight Houston feared might be enough to put him off women for the rest of his life.

With two expert slashes of the knife, she cut the oxen free of the leather traces. She laboriously climbed back on her horse, unrolled a whip that was wound around her pommel, gave it a sharp crack that sounded like a gunshot, and herded her patient beasts away.

No one said a word, least of all Houston, who knew when he was out matched. If he could only convince that woman to march with them and confront Santa Anna, he figured the war would be over in about five minutes.

While Mrs. Mann and her team rumbled out of sight, one of the gun crew asked, "General, what do we do now? These here cannon are stuck and stuck good."

Houston had half a mind to leave the damn things behind, but he knew that the men set great store by the Twin Sisters. It would be a serious loss to morale if he left them bogged down in the mud on the way to battle. And it probably *would* be handy to have something to fire back when Santa Anna's cannon fired at them. What did the Mexicans call their weapon; the Golden Standard? A ridiculous name, but it probably was better than being shot at by the brass standard.

Houston dismounted and fondly patted Saracen on the flank.

"Gentlemen, I suggest that for now we put our backs into it and give 'em a push," he said, calling for volunteers to help. "I'm sure there are enough of us to get the Sisters movin' again."

When he had sufficient men for the task, Houston anchored his boots in the mud and remembered just in time to put his good shoulder to the cannon. The other shoulder had never fully recovered from his gunshot wounds at Horseshoe Bend more than 20 years ago, although most of the time he didn't notice the weakness. The only visible sign was the mass of red and blue scar tissue across his shoulder and upper chest.

After several painful minutes while muscles strained and progress was measured by the inch, they finally worked the cannon free of the mud. While the men cheered their delight,

Houston arranged to have two teams of horses haul them the rest of the way, which meant that four unhappy men would have to walk.

Conrad Rohrer, the army's wagon master, a burley Pennsylvania Dutchman who Houston suspected of talking that terrifying woman out of her animals in the first place, rode up to the astonishing site of his mud-covered general supervising the cannon transport.

When Houston explained the situation, Rohrer, who did not have a problem colorfully expressing himself either, thundered that by God he would get those animals back from "that damned ugly cow who calls herself a female."

As the fuming Rohrer clattered away, Houston yelled that he'd best let the oxen go.

"I'm telling you, that woman will bite," he warned as the determined Rohrer rode out of sight.

No one saw Rohrer until much later, when he was caught trying to sneak back into camp after dark. The big Dutchman's face was scratched in long red lines, his shirt was torn to shreds, and the oxen remained with Mrs. Mann.

26

It was well after midnight and he had a small fire going, just enough for a little warmth and to throw light on their faces. With the exception of Houston, Karnes, Smith, and the guards patrolling the rim of the camp, virtually every man was asleep. Judging by the noise, virtually every man was snoring, too.

As usual, Houston wasn't sleeping much. Two or three hours a night still was all he could seem to manage. He knew that it would eventually catch up to him, but maybe not for a while yet. Karnes and Smith were known to be light sleepers, and he figured that they wouldn't mind being rousted out for a late-night – or early morning – conference, especially considering the subject.

He motioned to a pot over the fire. "There's coffee if you want it, if you want to call it that. At least it's hot and the right color."

When Smith and Karnes declined, Houston began.

"Gentleman, if it's at all possible we need to pick our ground carefully when we meet Santa Anna, who still thinks he's moving to block our retreat. In his arrogance, he doesn't know that we're chasing him now. I have some specific requirements in mind and I want you to ride ahead and find the right place for us."

Assessing at the scouts' curious but eager faces, Houston decided to rephrase his statement.

"I need *one* of you to find the right place. I don't want both of you gone at the same time. Knowing I don't have at least one of you around to call on gives me the night sweats. Whichever way you decide is fine with me, but only one of you goes and he can take as many men as he needs. I don't care if it's five or 50."

They grinned at that, as he knew they would. Reliable old Deaf Smith, a happily married man deep into middle age who never made a bad move, and the flamboyant, red-haired Henry Karnes, in the glowing prime of bachelor manhood; were any two men less alike? And were any two men better at what they did?

Houston paused for a moment, gathering his thoughts. He'd been pondering this for weeks, practically since they left Gonzales, and it seemed strange to finally express it.

"I want our camp to be hidden in the trees somewhere. I don't want the enemy to be able to see us; to see our size, our numbers. I don't know if Santa Anna's been told that we have cannon, but if he hasn't yet, I'd sure like to surprise him. There's no sense in showin' our cards before we have to."

"We'll also need a steady and reliable supply of water. By that I mean river or creek water, not the bayou and swamp shit that too many of our men drank and watched as their guts erupted. Not having water where he fought is part of what did poor Fannin in."

"The area needs to be confined, too, if that's possible. The bigger and more open the area of battle the greater the advantage of superior numbers. There's a decent chance that Santa Anna will have more men than we do and I don't want to run the risk of being flanked. The other thing is that, despite what Sherman thinks, their cavalry is better than ours and the less open space they have to work in the better it us for us. A wooded boundary would be all right. At least it would provide good cover for our riflemen. But men can get through woods, even cavalry. Water on most sides would be better."

"Finally, assuming if our camp is hidden, the perfect situation would be for Santa Anna to have to camp out in the open. What we can see can't surprise us."

Karnes rose from his place on the ground, picked up a tree limb, and poked at the slowly fading fire, stirring up a shower of sparks that drifted into the night air. He easily resumed his position on the ground with the suppleness of youth. Like Houston, he sat cross-legged.

Smith lay on the ground, with his head propped up with one hand. He complained that he couldn't sit like Houston and Karnes, at least not for very long, because "these old bones don't unwind the way they used to. It'd take me half a day to get back on my feet."

Although he didn't say so, Houston sympathized. He wasn't sure how fast he could unwind from this position either.

Seeing the incredulous looks on the scouts' faces after his recitation, he chuckled. "It possible that I ask too much? All I want is perfection."

Karnes spit a glob of tobacco juice on the fire, which resulted in a satisfying hiss.

"No harm in tellin' us what you need," he said. "We might not find everything you want, but there is plenty of water over that way, what with all the bayous, creeks, the rivers. Plenty of woods, too. A lot of it might not be too hard."

In his deliberate way, Smith thought it all through before nodding his agreement.

"It's just a matter of the right combination and lookin' long enough," he said.. "We'll see what we can do for you, general. Might have to settle, might not. Do the best we can."

"I know you will, Erastus. And you, Henry. You two have never let me down."

"And we don't intend to start now," Smith said. "You got our word on it."

27

THEY REACHED Buffalo Bayou just before noon.

Looking across the bayou, they could see the ashes of Harrisburg still smoldering. In a fit of anger or strategy – it didn't really matter which, Houston figured – Santa Anna had burned it to the ground.

Hearing the men curse when the saw what remained of the town, Houston only shrugged. "Have they already forgotten that *we* burned Gonzales and San Felipe?"

Houston and Hockley were mounted side by side as they looked over the bayou's brackish water. The general was astride Saracen, as usual, while Hockley rode the small black he favored. His aide's long legs seemed to almost touch the ground, but Hockey never seemed all that mindful of the figure he cut. Houston's believed that a man's mount said something about that man. Hockley figured that the right mount was the one that was easiest on his butt. Houston had spent enough time in the saddle to know that you could make a good argument either way.

"If you'll remember, sir, the men weren't too happy when we did burn Gonzales and San Felipe," Hockley replied. "I guess by now they figured out that it was done for a reason. Santa Anna probably did it just because he could."

"Maybe," Houston admitted. "Either way, the result's the same."

Houston took a deep breath and slowly let it out. "Hockley, I want you to assemble the men in one hour. It's about time I told them what the hell we're doin'."

"Yes, sir." But before he could put spur to horse, Houston spoke again, his head tilting toward Buffalo Bayou. "And once you get the word out, why don't you find us a way to get across that that water?"

The order pulled Hockley up short. "A way to get ... you mean boats, sir?" He didn't express the thought, but he wondered exactly where the general thought he was gong to find enough boats to transport more than 900 men, or even one boat."

Houston vastly enjoyed the sight as everyone f those thoughts passed across his aide's expressive face. He'd long ago decided that Hockley would make a terrible gambler. You'd know exactly what he had in his hand the moment he had it.

"Hockey nobody said it would be easy," Houston said as he wheeled Saracen and trotted away.

"It sure as hell isn't," muttered Hockley to his general's back, as close to mutiny as he had ever come.

————

As instructed, the men formed a hollow square. Virtually every man in the army was present, even the sick and injured, except for the guards, the patrols he had out to keep frm being surprised, and poor Hockley, who Houston figured at this very minute was busy trying to build a very large boat.

Knowing the drama of the moment, Houston waited until

the men were assembled before riding into the middle of the square on Saracen, with Tom Rusk at his side. He had decided to speak while mounted both for the dramatic effect and to allow his voice to carry further.

At first, there was a rustle among the men. Houston expected that. After all this time, how could it be otherwise?

After a moment, they settled down, eager to hear what their general had to say in this, his first formal speech to the troops. Along with his closing presentation to Congress when he was on trial for the beating of a Ohio congressman named William Stanbury, this would be the most important speech of his life. To his surprise, he was not at all nervous. It was a long time coming. He knew exactly what he had to say and how to say it.

As he knew from experience, a good speech was all about rhythm and timing. He started slowly.

A LOOK AT: THE LION AT BAY
SAM HOUSTON BOOK THREE

He's a Southern hero in a country on the edge of war.

Sam Houston has survived scandal, battlefields, and broken hearts. Now older, wearier, but no less stubborn, he finds himself at the center of a storm once more.

The Republic of Texas is gone, absorbed into the United States, and Houston is its first senator—a larger-than-life figure navigating the muddy streets of Washington, D.C., where deals are made in whispers and betrayals happen in broad daylight.

Back home, he's a husband and father with a growing family. In the capital, he's a Southern unionist and slaveholder who dares to defy the rising tide of secession—and pays the price. As the nation barrels toward civil war, Houston is out of step with allies, enemies, and even his own state. But he refuses to back down.

From fiery Senate debates to the Texas governor's mansion, Houston fights a lonely battle against disunion, knowing the cost will be high —and knowing, too, that some principles are worth the sacrifice.

AVAILABLE OCTOBER 2025

ABOUT THE AUTHOR

The author of eight novels, Robert Wisehart was born in Indianapolis, Indiana, and now is fortunate enough to live in Santa Fe, New Mexico.

In between Indianapolis and Santa Fe, he worked for many years as an award-winning reporter and columnist for newspapers in Florida, North Carolina, Louisiana and Northern and Southern California, plus occasional flirtations with radio and television as an on-air commentator. Such is the changing world that three of the four newspapers no longer exist.

Later, as a free-lance writer Wisehart did everything from write speeches to ghost books. He labored as a restaurant critic and for a brief time as a one of the dreaded horde of government consultants, two words that can mean almost anything but usually add up to not much. His work has appeared in more than 200 newspapers and 30 magazines, plus several digital outlets.

Wisehart and his wife, Dana, have been married for a lifetime and intend to make it a very long lifetime indeed. They have moved much, traveled well and Dana easily is the best thing that ever happened to him. Their two sons, Marc and Carl, live in New York City.